Chicago Public Library

W9-CIN-912

RU126228003

Dark water's embrace.

The bog bod___ ___ had foun_ ___ a man-sized, crumpled bag of leather—which in essence, it was. The acidic chemical stew of peat had tanned and preserved the skin, but the skeletal structure and most of the interior organs had dissolved away. Over the last several days in scraps of time between more pressing duties, I'd carefully cleaned away the worst of the peat clinging to the outside of the body, still hunched into its centuries-old fetal position. Now, like a gift, I was ready to unwrap the present given us by the bog.

I grunted as I turned the body so that it rested mostly on its back. "There appears to be a large tattoo on the chest and stomach—blue-black lines. Looks like a pictogram of some sort, but there's still a lot of peat obscuring it."

The remnant of the left leg was folded high up on the stomach, obscuring the tattoo. I lifted it carefully and moved it aside, revealing the groin. "Now that's interesting . . ."

I said nothing for several seconds. I was staring at the body, at the soft folds hiding the opening at the rear of the creature, not quite knowing whether to be angry. Trying to gather the shreds of composure. *Staring at myself in the mirror, forcing myself to look only at that other Anaïs's face, that contemplative, uncertain face lost in the fogged, spotted silver backing, and my gaze always inevitably, drifting lower . . .*

LITERATURE AND LANGUAGE LIBRARY
LITERAT___ ___ LANG___ DIVISION
4___ ___UTH STATE STREET
CHICAGO, ILLINOIS 60605

Avon Books are available at special quantity discounts for bulk purchases for sales promotions, premiums, fund raising or educational use. Special books, or book excerpts, can also be created to fit specific needs.

For details write or telephone the office of the Director of Special Markets, Avon Books, Dept. FP, 1350 Avenue of the Americas, New York, New York 10019, 1-800-238-0658.

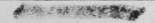

DARK WATER'S EMBRACE

STEPHEN LEIGH

This is a work of fiction. Names, characters, places, and incidents either are the product of the author's imagination or are used fictitiously. Any resemblance to actual events, locales, organizations, or persons, living or dead, is entirely coincidental and beyond the intent of either the author or the publisher.

AVON BOOKS
A division of
The Hearst Corporation
1350 Avenue of the Americas
New York, New York 10019

Copyright © 1998 by Stephen Leigh
Published by arrangement with the author
Visit our website at http://www.AvonBooks.com/Eos
Library of Congress Catalog Card Number: 97-94466
ISBN: 0-380-79478-0

All rights reserved, which includes the right to reproduce this book or portions thereof in any form whatsoever except as provided by the U.S. Copyright Law. For information address Avon Books.

First Avon Eos Printing: March 1998

AVON EOS TRADEMARK REG. U.S. PAT. OFF. AND IN OTHER COUNTRIES, MARCA REGISTRADA, HECHO EN U.S.A.

Printed in the U.S.A.

WCD 10 9 8 7 6 5 4 3 2 1

If you purchased this book without a cover, you should be aware that this book is stolen property. It was reported as "unsold and destroyed" to the publisher, and neither the author nor the publisher has received any payment for this "stripped book."

CHICAGO PUBLIC LIBRARY
LITERATURE AND LANGUAGE DIVISION
LITERATURE INFORMATION CENTER
400 SOUTH STATE STREET
CHICAGO, ILLINOIS 60605

To Becca and Guy
Because.

And, as ever, to Denise, with whom I've mingled jeans and
genes both.

ACKNOWLEDGMENTS

I would like to acknowledge *The Life and Death of a Druid Prince*, by Anne Ross and Don Robins (Simon & Schuster 1989)—an excellent book which gave me the initial "what if" impetus to this novel, however wildly divergent it actually is. Look up the book and read it—it's one of the most fascinating archeological detective stories you'll ever come across.

For some interesting speculation and insight into the causes of why species disappear, I would also like to recommend David M. Raup's *Extinction* (Norton, 1991).

I'd also like to thank Dr. Rebecca Levin for her input into the potential biology of the Miccail. Any errors of extrapolation and science are mine, not hers.

And if you're connected to the Internet, please check out my web page at www.sff.net/people/sleigh—you're always welcome to browse through!

A MICTLANIAN GLOSSARY

THE LANGUAGES OF MICTLAN,
HUMAN, AND MICCAIL:

The crew of the *Ibn Battuta*, drawn as they were from a multinational crew, adopted English as their *lingua franca*. However, most of the crew were at least bilingual, if not relatively fluent in three or four languages. Inevitably, words and phrases from other languages crept into their everyday speech. Well before the *Ibn Battuta* was launched, during the period when it was being constructed in orbit and the crew members were learning their roles, a subtle *patois* of many languages had come into common use among the crew and support personnel. The emerging language was almost a Creole, though the largest portion of the vocabulary derived from American English. By the time of their arrival at Mictlan, despite the ship-decades of LongSleep, this convention was firmly in place. New terms and descriptions might as easily be drawn from Cantonese, Japanese, Russian, Spanish, or Kiswahili as English, or even (as was the case with the world-name itself) an ancient Native American language such as Nahuatl. For the most part, we have stayed with English for the sake of readability. However, where it seemed appropriate, the terms used by the colonists have been appropriated here.

The sections from the viewpoint of the Miccail themselves contain words drawn from their own language, again where it seemed appropriate. As in Japanese (for instance), the Miccail created conglomerate words composed of smaller, monosyllabic nouns. Thus, "nasituda," the word for the carved stelae which were the first, most visible signs of the Miccail presence is Stone (*na*) Carved (*si*) Past (*tu*) Speak (*da*): literally, the Carved Stone that Speaks of History, or as we have (more romantically, perhaps, and certainly more freely) translated it here, Telling Stone.

The list of human and Miccail words below is by no means exhaustive, and is provided only to give some insight into derivations and meanings.

aabi	Miccail. Literally, "Ears hearing." An acknowledgment that you've heard and understood what was said to you.
AnglSaiye	Miccail. The Island, sacred home of the Sa
brais	Miccail. Literally, "Sun's Eye"; the pupilless third eye set high on the forehead of the Miccail. The brais cannot focus and the Miccail do not properly "see" with it. Instead, it serves as a "skylight" and warns them of sudden shifts in light which might signal the approach of a predator.
Chali	Miccail. The larger of Mictlan's two moons, dubbed Longago by the human colonists.
CieTiLa	Miccail. Literally, "Those Touched By The Gods." More simply, it means "The People," referring to the Miccail as a whole.
da	Human. Etymology uncertain. The closest meaning is perhaps "Uncle." Da refers to any male of a person's Family who is of a generation or more older.
danjite ikenai	Human, from Japanese: "Absolutely not"
dottó	Human, from Italian: a contraction of "dottore," or doctor. The English equivalent might be the colloquial "Doc."
Geeda	Human. Etymology uncertain. The eldest male of a Family
Geema	Human. Etymology uncertain. The eldest female of a Family
hai	Human, from Japanese: "Yes."
hakuchi	Human, from Japanese: "Idiot."
hand	Miccail counting: a "hand" equals four.
Ja	Miccail. A suffix indicating a female in servitude
Je	Miccail. A suffix indicating a male in servitude
jitu	Miccail. A narcotic drink used in Sa rituals.
kami	Human, from Japanese: a local spirit, either a minor deity or possibly the soul of a dead person.

kav — Miccail. An herbal tea

kasadi — Miccail. Ducklike amphibians who congregate on shorelines during their brief spring mating season

khudda — Human, from Syrian (vulgar): used as a profanity: human excrement

Kiria — Human, from Latin: Priest or Priestess. Probably derived from Kyrie.

komban wa — Human, from Japanese: "Good evening."

lavativo — Human, from Italian: "Lazybones"

mali cvijet — Human, from Serbo-Croatian: "Little Flower"—a term of endearment.

mam — Human. Etymology uncertain. "Mother." Since it was entirely unlikely that anyone could be certain of the father, there is no analogue word for the male parent on Mictlan.

marset — Miccail. A small mammalian animal hunted for both its food and fur.

mi — Human. Etymology uncertain. The closest meaning is perhaps "Aunt." It refers to any female of a person's Family who is older than you, and of whom you're not a direct descendant (i.e., not your mother, grandmother, etc.)

Miccail — Human, from Nahuatl: "The Dead." On Mictlan, the extinct race of sentient beings who perished a millennium before the arrival of the *Ibn Battuta*.

Mictlan — Human, from Nahuatl: "The Land of the Dead." In Aztec/Mayan creation myths, this is the Land of the Dead, from where the god Quetzalcoatl brought the bones of man. This was used as the world-name after the bones of a sentient race were found here.

mojo ljubav — Human, from Serbo-Croatian: "My love"

nasituda — Miccail. The Telling Stone of the Miccail, the carved stelae of crystal which are the most prominent remnants of that extinct race.

nei	Human. Etymology uncertain: "Absolutely not!"
Njia	Human, from Kiswahili: "The Way." This is the principal religious/philosophical belief system among the humans on Mictlan.
Quali	Miccail. The smaller of Mictlan's two moons, dubbed Faraway by the human colonists.
rezu	Human, from Japanese via Europe: a lesbian.
Sa	Miccail. A suffix indicating a Miccail midmale. Nearly all the rare midmales belonged to the Sa sect, a religious colony based on an island.
shangaa	Miccail. The long, caftanlike robe that was the main item of clothing worn by the Miccail. Shangaa, woven from the pulp of a native plant, were dyed many bright colors, and varied from plain, utilitarian robes to fine ceremonial costumes.
sib	Human, from English: "sibling." On Mictlan, a sib is anyone of your Family of the same generation, regardless of who the mother was.
Ta	Miccail. A suffix for the dominant female in a Miccail tribe, also known as the Old-Mother.
Te	Miccail. a suffix indicating that the person is the OldFather of a Miccail tribe, the dominant male.
terduva	Miccail. A segment of time equal to 512 (or $8 \times 8 \times 8$) years. The Miccail, with hands consisting of three fingers and a thumb, counted in base eight.
Ti	Miccail. The suffix used for a deity.
Tlilipan	Human, from Nahuatl: "place of black water." Name given to a peat-stained lake near the colony site.
Tu	Miccail. The suffix used to designate the head of the Community of Sa.

una tortillera   Human, from Spanish: in extremely vulgar usage, a lesbian.

VeiSaTi   Miccail. One of the gods of the Miccail, the one most sacred to the sect of the Sa.

verrechat   Human, from French: "glass cat." A small, catlike marsupial with transparent or lightly tinted skin and muscles. Sometimes domesticated.

wizards   Human. A contraction of "winged lizards"— a type of flying reptile found near the human settlement.

Xa   Miccail. A suffix indicating a female of the free caste

Xe   Miccail. A suffix indicating a male of the free caste

xeshai   Miccail. Literally, "Second Fight"—a ritual-bound two person combat that was the usual method for solving severe disagreements between Miccail tribes. Each Te or Ta would choose a champion from among the Xe or Xa to represent them. In rare cases, *xeshai* might be group combat, but even then there were specific rules limiting how the conflict would be handled.

I suspect that if humankind had never known sex, we would have invented it anyway: the women to celebrate friendship, and the men to celebrate themselves.

—Gabriel Rusack

DARK WATER'S EMBRACE

DISCOVERIES

CONTEXT:
Elena Koda-Schmidt

THE AUTUMN DAY WAS AS HOT AS ANY IN RECENT memory. The temperature was nearly 10°C, and Elena paused to unbutton her sweater and wipe away the sweat that threatened to drip into her eyes. Near the tree line bordering the river a kilometer away, the dark waters of a pond glittered in the sun: Tlilipan, it was called, "the place of black water." The peat-stained shallow lake was the last vestige of a much larger parent, now just a marshy wetland. Further down the peat bog, Elena could see Faika Koda-Shimmura and Aldhelm Martinez-Santos—they were kissing, a long, oblivious embrace that made Elena feel vaguely jealous, watching. Faika was ten and had reached her menarche.

Elena suspected that her brother Wan-Li was going to be disappointed when she told him. Wan-Li had spent the night in the Koda-Shimmura compound with Faika a few days before. It seemed he hadn't quite made the impression he'd thought he had. Elena remembered her own menarche year, and how she'd experimented with her new sexual freedom.

The cart was nearly full of peat; Elena leaned her shovel against the wheel and rubbed her protruding stomach with callused hands. She loved the swelling, surprising curve of her belly, loved the weight of it, the feeling of being centered and rooted. Her roundness made her believe that despite the odds, *her* baby would be perfect. *Her* baby would live and give her grandchildren to dandle on her knee when she was past childbearing herself. She stroked the hard sphere of her womb and the baby kicked in response. Elena laughed.

"Now you be still, little one. It's bad enough without you stomping on my bladder. Mama's still got a lot of work to do before we get home."

With a sigh, Elena picked up the shovel and prepared to attack the peat once more. She was working an old face, several feet down in the bog where the peat was rich, thick,

3

and as dark as old Gerard's face. She lifted the spade.
Stopped.

A flap of something leathery and brown like stained wood protruded from the earth, about a foot up on the wall of the ancient marsh. Elena crouched down, grunting with the unaccustomed bulk of her belly. She peered at the fold of leather, prodding it with the tip of her shovel to pull a little more out of the moss.

Elena gasped and dropped the shovel. Protruding from the appendage, squashed and compressed by the weight of centuries of peat, was a hand with four fingers, the tip of each finger a wide knob capped with a recessed claw. The shock sent Elena stepping backward. The shovel's handle tangled between her legs, tripping her. She put her hands out instinctively to protect her stomach. She grunted with the impact, and the handle slammed against her knee. For a moment, she just lay there, taking inventory. The child jumped inside her, and she breathed again.

"Faika—" she began, but the shout came out entangled in the breath. She thought of how she must look, sprawled in the wet dirt and staring at the apparition in the peat, and laughed at herself.

"What a sight!" she told the child in her womb. "You'd think your mother was sure the boggin was going to get up and walk out of there," she said. She stood, brushing uselessly at her stained trousers and grimacing with the bruised, protesting knee.

As she stood, she saw movement from the corner of her eye. A figure shifted in the small stand of globe-trees a hundred meters away. "Faika? Aldhelm?" Elena called, but the shadowy form—almost lost in tree-shadow—moved once more, and she knew it wasn't either of the two. She could feel it, watching, staring at her. *A grumbler?* she thought, wondering if the rifle was still in the cart, but in the instant she glanced away to check the weapon, the shadow was gone.

There was no one there. The sense of being observed was gone.

Elena shivered, hugging herself. "Baby, your mother's seeing ghosts now," she said. She glanced back at the hand hanging from the peat. "I think I just saw your *kami*," she told it. "Don't worry, I'm not going to do anything nasty to you. I'll leave that to Anaïs. Knowing her, she'll *enjoy* it."

4

She took a deep breath, and looked again at the copse of trees. "Faika! Aldhelm!" Elena shouted. "If you two can stop fondling each other for a minute or so, I think you should come here and look at this."

VOICE:
Anaïs Koda-Levin the Younger

"SO . . . ARE YOU PREGNANT YET, ANAÏS?"

I hate that question. I always have the wrong answer.

No. I'm not.

"Give it a rest, Ghost."

"Everything's still the same, is it? You *are* still trying, aren't you? If we could only get you up here so we could *see. . . ."*

I felt the old emotional garbage rising with Ghost's questioning: the anger, the bitterness, the self-loathing. I forced the gorge down, packing the filth down behind that internal wall, but it was an effort. Our ancient steel surgical instruments, worn to a satin patina by over a century of use and constant sterilization, beat a raucous percussion on the tray I was holding. "Ghost—"

"Sorry, Anaïs. No need to get irritated. As the repository of Mictlan's history . . ."

There are times when I wish I knew programming well enough to tone down Ghost's assertiveness. "Shut up, Ghost."

This time around, Ghost looked like an old blind man, hunched over an ornate glass cane that was as swirled and frosted as a Miccail stele. His sightless, ice-blue eyes stared somewhere past my right shoulder into the back corner of the coldroom lab. The outline of his body sparkled and flared disconcertingly, and his legs were implanted in the polished whitewood planking past his ankles.

"Ghost, Hui and I put a new floor in here since the last time. You look like you're wading in wood, and it's really

5

disconcerting. Can you shift your image up about a dozen centimeters?"

"Oh, now that we're on the subject of sex and reproduction, you want to change it? Anaïs, I know it's no comfort to you, but if it were possible to reach the *Ibn Battuta*, a resonance scan or even an ultrasound would answer a lot of questions, and we could—"

"Drop it, Ghost. Drop it right now."

This time, I made no effort to hide the anger. Ghost reminded me too much of the sympathy, the false reassurances given to me by my sibs, by my *mam* Maria. They look into my room and see my clothing draped carefully over the huge mirror (which had once belonged to Rebecca Koda-Levin herself), the shirts and pants arranged so that the mirror reflects nothing, and they don't understand the significance of what they're seeing.

The old man sighed. The image, sparking, raised up until the soles of his feet were almost even with the floor. "Better?"

"It'll do."

"You're going to have to describe what you're seeing," Ghost said. "Since you've had the ill grace not to put a video feed in here."

"Quit complaining." My voice was muffled through the gauze mask I was tying behind my head, and my breath clouded in the cold air. "We put the feed in; the line was bad. No one's had a chance to fix it yet—it's not exactly high priority. Maybe next time."

"But I'm curious *now*," Ghost persisted. "I don't have much time this orbit. Come on—you're as slow as your Geema."

I sniffed. A strand of hair had made an escape from the surgical cap; I brushed it out of my eyes. "Maybe that's why they named me for her, huh?"

The retort was weak but it was the best I had at the moment. I turned back to the examination table and its strange contents. The bog body Elena had found lay there like a man-sized, crumpled bag of leather—which, in essence, it was. The acidic chemical stew of the peat had tanned and preserved the skin, but the skeletal structure and most of the interior organs had dissolved away. Over the last several days, in scraps of time between other, more pressing duties, I'd carefully cleaned away the worst of the peat clinging to the outside of the body, still hunched into its centuries-old

6

fetal position. Now, like a gift, I was ready to unwrap the present given us by the bog.

Every time I'd looked at the body, I'd felt the same rush of adrenaline I felt now, a sense of standing in front of something . . . I don't know . . . maybe *sacred* is the best word. Old and venerable, certainly. I was almost inclined to believe Elena's tale about seeing a *kami* watching her when she'd found it.

After all, it was the bones of this race's dead that had given rise to the name given to the planet: Mictlan, suggested by the lone Mexican crewmember of the *Ibn Batutta*. Mictlan was the Aztec land of the dead, where the god Quetzalcoatl found the bones of humankind—and now, where the bones of another dead culture had been found. The race itself were christened the Miccail—"the Dead," in the Nahautl language. In the years following, a few Miccailian burial sites had been explored. Not that the excavations told us much about the Miccail, since they cremated their dead before they buried the calcined and charred bones—a rite we'd borrowed from them for our own dead. The strange, whorled spires the Miccail had left behind on the northern continent, sticking out of Mictlan's rocky soil like faerie cathedrals of dull glass and carved with images of themselves, had been photographed and documented; it was from these that we learned the most about the extinct race. More would have been done, probably, but the near destruction and crippling of the *Ibn Battuta* not six months after the colonists' arrival and the resultant death of nearly all the crew members had suddenly, radically, and permanently shifted everyone's priorities.

Basically, it was more important to scrape an existence from Mictlan than to try to decipher the mystery of our world's previous inhabitants

I suppose I could appreciate my ancestors' sentiments. Priorities hadn't changed much in the century since the accident. Survival was still far more important than any anthropological exploration. No one wanted Mictlan to harbor the scattered bones of *two* extinct, sentient races. I suppose we have the deliberate uncuriosity of the matriarchs and patriarchs to thank for our being here at all.

For one reason or another, though, I don't seem to be much like them. In so many ways. . . .

"Are you ready to record, Ghost?"

"I'd have much more to analyze with video."

7

I waited. A moment later, Ghost sighed. The ancient's body dissolved into static for a moment, then returned as a young woman in an *Ibn Battuta* officer's uniform, though a fanciful, brightly-colored scarf was tied over her eyes like a blindfold. The voice changed also, from an elderly male quaver to a female soprano. "Recording into *Ibn Battuta* memory. Audio only log: 101 September 41. The voice is Anaïs Koda-Levin the Younger, Generation Six. Go ahead, Anaïs."

I gave Ghost a sidewise look, swearing—as I had a few hundred times before—that I'd never understand why Gabriela had programmed her AI with such a quirky sense of humor and strange set of idiosyncracies. "All right. This is another examination of the Miccail body found in the peat bog—and this will be very cursory, I'm afraid, since I'm on duty in the clinic tonight. Ghost, you can download my previous recordings from the Mictlan library."

"It's already done. Go on, Ana, you have my undivided attention."

I knew that wasn't true—there were still three other working projectors scattered among the compounds, and Ghost was no doubt talking with people at each of them at the moment, as well as performing the systems work necessary to keep our patchwork and shrinking network of century-old terminals together, but it was a nice lie. I shook my hair back from my eyes once more and leaned over the table.

Imagine someone unzipping his skin, crumpling it up, and throwing the discarded epidermis in a corner like an old suit—that's what the corpse looked like. On its side, the body was drawn up like someone cowering in fear, the right arm folded around its back, the left thrown over the right shoulder like a shawl. The head was bowed down into the chest, crushed flat and turned to the left. I could see the closed lid of the right eye and the translucent covering of the central "eye" high on the forehead. A mane of dark, matted hair ran from the back of the bald, knobbed skull and halfway down the spine.

I gently pulled down the right leg, which was tucked up against the body. The skin moved grudgingly; I had to go slowly to avoid tearing it, moistening the skin occasionally with a sponge. Tedious work.

"Most of the body is intact," I noted aloud after a while, figuring that Ghost was going to complain if I didn't start talking soon. "From the spinal mane and the protrusions around the forehead, it's one of the type Gabriela designated as 'Nomads.' If I recall correctly, she believed that since the carvings of Nomads disappear from the Miccail's stelae in the late periods, these were a subspecies that went extinct a millennium or so before the rest of the Miccail."

"You've been studying things you've been told to stay away from."

"Guilty as charged. So that makes the body—what?—two thousand years old?"

"No later than that," Ghost interrupted, "assuming Gabriela's right about the stelae. We'll have a better idea when we get the estimates from the peat samples and measurements. Máire's still working on them."

"Sounds fine. I'll check with her in the next few days."

I was lost in the examination now, seeing nothing but the ancient corpse in front of me. A distant part of me noted that my voice had gone deeper and more resonant, no longer consciously pitched high—we all have our little idiosyncracies, I suppose. "Two thousand or more years old, then. The body evidently went naked into the lake that later became the bog—there's no trace of any clothing. That may or may not be something unusual. The pictographs on the Miccail stelae show ornate costumes in daily use, on the Nomads as well as the rest, so it's rather strange that this one's naked. . . . Maybe he was swimming? Anyway, we're missing the left leg a half meter down from the hip and . . ."

The right leg, boneless and twisted, lay stretched on the table. Fragments of skin peeled from the stump of the ankle like bark from a whitewood. ". . . the right foot a few centimeters above the ankle. A pity—I'd like to have seen that central claw on the foot. Looks like the leg and foot decayed off the body sometime after it went into the lake. Wouldn't be surprised if they turn up somewhere else later."

I straightened the right arm carefully, laying it down on the table, moving slowly from shoulder to wrist. "Here's one hand—four fingers, not five. Wonder if they counted in base eight? These are really long phalanges, though the metacarpals must have been relatively short. The pads at the end of each digit still have vestiges of a recessed claw—would have been a nasty customer in a fight. There's webbing almost halfway up the finger; bet they swam well. And this thumb . . . it's highly opposed and much longer than a human's. From the folds in the skin, I'd guess that it had an extra articulation, also."

I grunted as I turned the body so that it rested mostly on

its back. "There appears to be a large tattoo on the chest and stomach—blue-black lines. Looks like a pictogram of some sort, but there's still a lot of peat obscuring it, and I'll have to make sure that this isn't some accidental postmortem marking of some kind. I'll leave that for later...."

The remnant of the left leg was folded high up on the stomach, obscuring the tattoo. I lifted it carefully and moved it aside, revealing the groin. "Now *that's* interesting...."

"What?" Ghost asked. "I'm a blind AI, remember?"

I exhaled under the surgical mask, resisting the urge to rise to Ghost's baiting. "The genitalia. There's a scaly, fleshy knob, rather high on the front pubis. I suppose that's the penis analogue for the species, but it doesn't look like normal erectile tissue or a penile sheath. No evidence of anything like testicles—no scrotal sac at all. Maybe they kept it inside."

"They're aliens, remember? Maybe they didn't *have* one."

I accepted Ghost's criticism with a nod. She was right—I was lacing some heavy anthropomorphism into my speculations. "Maybe. There's a youngpouch on the abdomen, though, and I haven't seen any Mictlanian marsupialoids where both sexes *had* the pouch. Maybe in the Miccail both male and female suckled the young." I lifted the leg, turning the body again with an effort. "There's a urethra further down between the legs, and an anus about where you'd expect it—"

I stopped, dropping the leg I was holding. It fell to the table with a soft thud. I breathed. I could feel a flush climbing my neck, and my vision actually shivered for a moment, disorientingly.

"Anaïs?"

"It's ..." I licked suddenly dry lips. Frowned. "There's what looks to be a vaginal opening just below the base of the spine, past the anus."

"A hermaphrodite," Ghost said, her voice suddenly flat. "Now there's serendipity for you, eh?"

I said nothing for several seconds. I was staring at the body, at the soft folds hiding the opening at the rear of the creature, not quite knowing whether to be angry. Trying to gather the shreds of composure. *Staring at myself in the mirror, forcing myself to look only at that other Anaïs's face, that contemplative, uncertain face lost in the fogged, spotted silver backing, and my gaze always, inevitably, drifting lower ....*

10

The Miccail body was an accusation, a mockery placed just for me by whatever gods ruled Mictlan.

"Gabriela speculated about the sexuality of the Nomads," Ghost continued. "There were notes in her journals. She collected rubbings of some rather suggestive carvings on the Middle Period stelae. In fact, in a few cases she referred to the Nomads as 'midmales' because the stelae were ambiguous as to which they might be. It's all scanned in the database—call it up."

"I've read some of Gabriela's journals—the public ones, anyway. Gabriela said a lot of strange things about the Miccail—and everything else on this world. Doesn't make her right."

"Give poor Gabriela a break. No one else was particularly interested in the Miccail after the accident. The first generation had more pressing problems than an extinct race. As an archeologist/anthropologist she was—just like you, I might add—a dilettante, a rank amateur."

"And she was your lead programmer, right? That explains a lot about *you*."

"It's also why I'm still working. Ana, I'm running out of time here."

"All right."

I took another long breath, trying to find the objective, aloof Anaïs the bog body had banished. The leg had fallen so that the tattered end of the ankle hung over the edge of the table. I placed it carefully back into position and didn't look at the trunk of the body or the mocking twinned genitals. Instead, I moved around the table, going to the Nomad's head. Carefully, I started prying it from the folded position it had held for centuries.

"Looks like she . . . he . . . ," I stopped. Ghost waited. My jaw was knotted; I forced myself to relax. *Do this goddamn thing and get it over with. Put the body back in the freezer and forget about it.* "She didn't die of drowning. There's a large wound on the back of the skull. Part crushing, part cutting, like a blunt axe, and it probably came from behind. I'll bet we'll find that's the cause of death, though I guess it's possible she was thrown into the lake still alive. I'm moving the head back to its normal position now. Hey, what's this . . . ?"

I'd lifted the chin of the Miccail. Trapped deep in the folds of the neck was a thin, knotted cord, a garrote, pulled so tightly against the skin that I could see that the windpipe

11

had closed under the pressure. "He was strangled as well."

"He? I thought it was a she."

I exhaled in exasperation. "God*damn* it, Ghost . . ."

"Sorry," Ghost apologized. She didn't sound particularly sincere. "Axed, strangled, *and* drowned," Ghost mused. "Wonder which happened first?"

"Somebody really wanted him dead. Poor thing." I looked down at the flattened, peat-darkened features, telling myself that I was only trying to see in them some reflection of the Miccail's mysterious life. This Miccail was a worse mirror than the one in my room. Between the pressure-distorted head and the long Miccail snout, the wide-set eyes, the light-sensitive eyelike organ at the top of the head, the nasal slits above the too-small, toothless mouth, it was difficult to attribute any human expression to the face. I sighed. "Let's see if we can straighten out the other arm—"

"Ana," Ghost interrupted, "you have company on the way, I'm afraid—"

"Anaïs!"

The shout came from outside, in the clinic's lobby. A few seconds later, Elio Allen-Shimmura came through the lab doors in a burst. His dark hair was disheveled, his black eyes worried. The hair and eyes stood out harshly against his light skin, reddened slightly from the cold northwest wind. His plain, undistinguished features were furrowed, creasing the too-pale forehead under the shock of bangs and drawing the ugly, sharp planes of his face even tighter. He cast a glance at the bog body; I moved between Elio and the Miccail. Some part of me didn't want him to see, didn't want anyone to see.

Elio didn't seem to notice. He glanced quickly to the glowing apparition of Ghost. "Is that you, Elio?" Ghost asked. "I can't see through this damn blindfold." Ghost grinned under the parti-colored blindfold.

Elio smiled in return, habitually, an expression that just touched the corners of his too-thin lips and died. "It's me." Something was bothering Elio; he couldn't stand still, shuffling from foot to foot as if he were anxious to be somewhere else. I'd often noticed that reaction in my presence, but at least this time I didn't seem to be the cause of it. Elio turned away from Ghost. "Anaïs, has Euzhan been in here?"

"Haven't seen her, El." *Your Geeda Dominic doesn't exactly encourage your Family's children to be around me*, I wanted to add, but didn't. With my own Family having no children at

12

the moment, if I had a favorite kid in the settlement, it would be Euzhan, a giggling, mischievous presence. Euzhan liked me, liked me with the uncomplicated trust of a child; liked me—I have to admit—with the same unconscious grace that her mother had possessed. It was impossible not to love the child back. I began to feel a sour stirring in the pit of my stomach.

"Damn! I was hoping . . ." Elio's gaze went to the door, flicking away from me.

"El, what's going on?"

He spoke to the air somewhere between Ghost and me. "It's probably nothing. Euz is missing from the compound, has been for an hour. Dominic's pretty frantic. We'll probably find her hiding in the new building, but . . ."

I could hear the forced nonchalance in Elio's voice; that told me that they'd already checked the obvious places where a small child might hide. A missing child, in a population as small as ours, was certainly cause for immediate concern—Dominic, the current patriarch of the Allen-Shimmura family, would have sent out every available person to look for the girl. Elio frowned and shook his head. "All right. You're in the middle of something, I know. But if you do see her—"

His obvious distress sparked guilt. "This has waited for a few thousand years. It can certainly wait another hour or two. I'll come help. Just give me a few minutes to put things away and scrub."

"Thanks. We appreciate it." Elio glanced again at the Miccail's body, still eclipsed behind me, then gave me a small smile before he left. I was almost startled by that and returned the smile, forgetting that he couldn't see it behind the mask. As he left, I slid the examining table back into the isolation compartment, then went to the sink and began scrubbing the protective brownish covering of thorn-vine sap from my hands.

"A bit of interest there?" Ghost ventured.

"You're blind, remember?"

"Only visually. I'm getting excellent audio from your terminal. Let me play it back—you'll hear how your voice perked up—"

"Elio's always been friendly enough to me, that's all. I'm not interested; he's *definitely* not, or he hides it awfully well. Besides, El is . . ." *Ugly*, I almost said, and realized how that would sound, coming from me. *His eyes are nice, and his*

13

hands. But his face—the eyes are set too close together, his nose is too long and the mouth too large. His skin is a patchwork of blotches. And the one time we tried . . . "At least he doesn't look at me like . . . like . . ." I hated the way I sounded, hated the fact that I knew Ghost was recording it all. I hugged myself, biting my lower lip. "Look, I really don't want to talk about this."

Ghost flickered. Her face morphed into lines familiar from holos of the Matriarchs: Gabriela. "Making sense of an attraction is like analyzing chocolate. Just enjoy it, and to hell with the calories." The voice was Gabriela's, too: smoky, husky, almost as low as mine.

"You're quoting."

"And you're evading." A line of fire-edged darkness sputtered down Ghost's figure from head to foot as the image began to break up. "Doesn't matter—I'm also drifting out of range. See you in three days this time. I should have a longer window then. Make sure you document everything about the Miccail body."

"I will. You get me those age estimates from Máire's uploads when you can."

"Promise." Static chattered in Ghost's voice; miniature lightning storms crackled across her body. She disappeared, then returned, translucent. I could see the murdered Nomad's body through her. "Go help Elio find Euzhan."

"I will. Take care up there, Ghost."

A flash of light rolled through Ghost's image. She went two-dimensional and vanished utterly.

CONTEXT:
Bui Allen-Shimmura

"BUI, GEEDA DOMINIC WANTS YOU. NOW."

Bui felt his skin prickle in response, like spiders scurrying up his spine. He straightened up, closing the vegetable bin door. Euzhan wasn't there, wasn't in any of her usual hiding places. Bui looked at Micah's lopsided face, and could see that there was no good news there. He asked anyway. "Did anyone find her?"

Micah shook his head, his lips tight. "Not yet," he answered, his voice blurred with his cleft palate. "Geeda's sent Elio out to alert the other Families and get them to help search."

"*Khudda.*" Bui didn't care that *da* Micah heard him cursing. The way Bui figured it, he couldn't get into any more trouble than he was already in. If he found Euzhan now, he might just kill the girl for slipping away while he was responsible for watching her. It wasn't fair: He'd be ten in half a year. At his age, he should have been out working the fields with the rest, not babysitting.

"How's Geeda?" he asked Micah.

"In as foul a mood as I've ever seen. You'd better get up there fast, boy."

Bui's shoulders sagged. He almost started to cry, sniffing and wiping his nose on his sleeve. "Go on," Micah told him. "Get it over with."

He went.

Geeda Dominic was in the common room of the Allen-Shimmura compound, staring out from the window laser-chiseled from the stone of the Rock. A dusty sunbeam threw Dominic's shadow on the opposite wall. Bui noticed immediately that no one else from the Family was in the room. That didn't bode well, since the others sometimes managed to keep Dominic's infamous temper in check. "Geeda?" Bui said tremulously. "Micah said you—"

Dominic was the eldest of the Allen-Shimmura family, a venerable eighty, but he turned now with a youth born of anger. His cane, carved by the patriarch Shigetomo himself, with a knobbed head of oak all the way from Earth, slashed air and slammed into Bui's upper arm. Surprise and pain made Bui cry out, and the blow was hard enough to send him sprawling on the rug.

"*Hakuchi!*" Dominic shouted at him, the cane waving in Bui's face like a club. "You fool!"

Bui clutched his arm, crying openly now. "Geeda, it wasn't my fault. Hizo, he'd fallen and skinned his knees, and when I finished with him, Euzhan—"

"Shut up!" The cane *whoomped* as it flashed in front of his face. "You listen to me, boy. If Euzhan is hurt or ... or ..."
Bui knew the word that Dominic wouldn't say. *Dead.* Fear reverberated in Bui's head, throbbing in aching syncopation

with the pain in his arm. "You better hope they find her safe, boy, or I'll have you goddamn shunned. I swear I will. No one will talk to you again. You'll be cast out of the Family. You'll find your own food or you'll starve."

"No, Geeda, please . . ." Bui shivered.

"Get out of here," Dominic roared. His hand tightened around the shaft of his cane, trembling. "Get out of here and find her. Don't bother coming back until you do. You understand me, boy?"

"Yes, Geeda Dominic. I'm . . . I'm sorry . . . I'm awful sorry . . ." Bui, still sobbing, half crawled, half ran from the room.

Dominic's cane clattered against the archway behind Bui as he went through.

VOICE:
Anaïs Koda-Levin the Younger

"EUZHAN! DAMN IT, CHILD. . . ."
    I exhaled in frustration, my voice hoarse from calling. Elio sagged tiredly near me. He rubbed the glossy stock of his rifle with fingers that seemed almost angry. "It's getting dark," he said. "It's near SixthHour. She'll come out from wherever she's hiding as soon as she notices. She always wants the light on in the creche, and she'll be getting hungry by now. She'll be out. I know it."

Elio wasn't convincing even himself. There was a quick desperation in his voice. I understood it all too well. All of us did. Our short history's full of testimonials to this world's whims—as our resident historian, Elio probably understood that better than I did.

Mictlan had not been a kind world for the survivors of *Ibn Batutta*. Two colonies—one on each of Mictlan's two continents—had been left behind after the accident that had destroyed most of the mothership. The colonies quickly lost touch with each other when a massive, powerful hurricane raked the southern colony's continent in the first year of ex-

16

ile, and they never resumed radio contact with us or with Ghost on the *Ibn Battuta*.

Another storm had nearly obliterated our northern colony in Year 23, killing six of the original nine crewmembers here. I suppose that was our historical watershed, since that disaster inalterably changed the societal structure, giving rise to what became the Families. Local diseases mutated to attack our strange new host bodies, stalking the children especially—the Bloody Cough alone killed two children in five by the time they reached puberty. I know: I see the bodies and do the autopsies. There are the toothworms or the tree-leapers or the grumblers; there are the bogs and the storms and the bitter winters; there are accidents and infections and far, far too many congenital defects. Most of them are bad enough that nature itself takes care of them: miscarriages, stillbirths, nonviable babies who are born and die within a few days or a few months—which is why none of the Families name a child before his or her first birthday. I also know the others—the ones who lived but who are marked with the stamp of Mictlan.

I knew *them* very well.

The rate of viable live births—for whatever reason: a side effect of the LongSleep, or some unknown factor in the Mictlan environment—was significantly lower among the ship members and their descendants than for the general population of Earth. Just over a century after being stranded on Mictlan, our human population nearly matched the year; there'd been no growth for the last quarter of a century. Too many years, deaths outnumbered births.

Mictlan was not a sweet, loving Motherworld. She was unsympathetic and unremittingly harsh.

I knew that Elio's imagination was calculating the same dismal odds mine was. This was no longer just a child hiding away from her *mi* or *da*, not this late, not this long.

Euzhan was four. I'd seen the girl in the clinic just a few days ago—an eager child, still awkward and lisping, and utterly charming. Ochiba, Euzhan's mother, had once been my best—hell, one of my only—friends. What we'd had. . . .

Anyway, Euzhan had been a difficult birth, a breech baby. All of Ochiba's births were difficult; her pelvis was narrow, barely wide enough to accommodate a baby's head. On Earth, she would have been an automatic cesarean, but not here, not when any major operation is an open invitation for some postoperative infection. I could have gone in. Ochiba

17

told me she'd go with whatever I decided. Ochiba had delivered three children before—with long, difficult labors, each time. I made the decision to let her go, and she—finally—delivered twelve hours later.

But Ochiba's exhaustion after the long labor gave an opportunistic respiratory virus its chance—Ochiba died three days after Euzhan's birth on 97 LastDay. Neither Hui Koda-Schmidt, the colony's other "doctor," nor I had been able to break the raging fever or stop the creeping muscular paralysis that followed. Our medical database is quite extensive, but is entirely Earth-based. On Mictlan-specific diseases, there's only the information that we colonists have entered, and I was all too familiar with that. Ghost had been out of touch, the *Ibn Battuta's* unsynchronized orbit trapping the AI on the far side of Mictlan. I don't have the words to convey the utter helpless impotence I'd felt, watching Ochiba slowly succumb, knowing that I was losing someone I loved.

Knowing that maybe, just maybe, my decision had been the reason she died.

I'd been holding Ochiba's hand at the end. I cried along with her Family, and Dominic—grudgingly—had even asked me to speak for Ochiba at her Burning.

A damn small consolation.

Euzhan, Ochiba's third named child, was especially precious to Dominic, the head of Family Allen-Shimmura. Euz was normal and healthy. As we all knew too well, any child was precious, but one such as Euzhan was priceless. The growing fear that something tragic had happened to Euzhan was a black weight on my soul.

"Who was watching Euz?"

"Bui," Elio answered. "Poor kid. Dominic'll have him skinned alive if Euz is hurt."

Nearly all of the Allen-Shimmura family were out searching for Euzhan now, along with many from the other Families. The buildings were being scoured one more time; a large party had gone into the cultivated fields to the southeast of the compound and were prowling the rows of white-bean stalks and scarlet faux-wheat. Elio and I had gone out along the edge of Tlilipan. I'd been half-afraid we'd see Euzhan's tiny footprints pressed in the mud flats along the pond's shore, but there'd been nothing but the cloverleaf tracks of skimmers. That didn't mean that Euzhan hadn't fallen into one of the patches of wet marsh between the colony and Tlilipan, or that a prowling grumbler hadn't come

18

across her unconscious body and dragged her off, still half-alive, to a rocky lair along the river. . . .

I forced the thoughts away. I shivered under my sweater and shrugged the strap of the medical kit higher on my shoulder. I've never been particularly religious, but I found myself praying to whatever *kami* happened to be watching.

Just let her be all right. Let her come toddling out of some forgotten hole in the compound, scared and dirty, but unharmed.

The sun was prowling the tops of the low western hills, the river trees painting long, grotesque shadows which rippled over the bluefern-pocked marshland. Not far away was the pit where we'd dug the Miccail body from the peat. Behind the trees, the chill breeze brought the thin, faint sound of voices from below the Rock, calling for Euzhan. I turned to look, squinting back up the rutted dirt road. There, a tall blackness loomed against the sky: the Rock. The first generation had carved a labyrinth of tunnels in the monolithic hill of bare stone perched alongside the river; from the various openings, we'd added structures that poked out like wood, steel, and glass growths on the stone, so that the Families lived half in and half out of the granite crag. Now, in its darkness, the familiar lights of the Family compounds glistened.

The Rock. Home to all of us.

"Let's keep looking," I told Elio. "We still have time before it gets too dark."

Elio nodded. Where his light skin met the dark cloth of his shirt there was a knife-sharp contrast that stood out even in the dusk. "Fine. We should spread out a bit. . . ."

Elio looked so forlorn that I found myself wanting to move closer to him, to hug him. As much as I might have denied it to Ghost, the truth was that Elio was someone I genuinely liked. Maybe it was because he was so plain, with that pale, blotchy skin, his off-center mouth and wide nose, and his gawky, nervous presence. Elio was not one of the popular men, not one of those who spend every possible night in some woman's room, but we talked well, and I liked the way he walked and the fact that one side of his mouth went higher than the other when he smiled. I liked the warmth in his voice.

He was tapping the rifle stock angrily, staring out into the marsh. I touched his arm; he jerked away. Under the deep ridges of his brows, his black eyes glinted. I could read nothing in them, couldn't tell what he was thinking.

19

"Let's go find Euz," I said.

The light had slid into a deep gold, almost liquid. The sun was half lost behind slopes gone black with shadow. If we were going to continue searching, we'd have to go back soon for lights. Elio and I moved slowly around the marsh's edge, calling Euz's name and peering under the low-hanging limbs of the amberdrop trees, brushing aside the sticky, purplish leaves. Darkness crept slowly over the landscape, the temperature dropping as rapidly as the sun. The marsh steamed in the cooling air, the evening fog already cloud-thick near the river. Our breaths formed small thunderheads before us. Neither of the moons—the brooding Longago or its smaller, fleeter companion Faraway—were up yet. At the zenith, the stars were hard, bright points set in satin, though a faint trace of deep blue lingered at the horizon. Near the compound, outside the fences, someone had lit a large bonfire; the breeze brought the scent of smoke.

"El? It's way past SixthHour, and it's getting too dark to see. . . ."

"All right," Elio sighed. "I guess we might as well—"

Before he could finish, a grumbler's basso growl shivered the evening quiet, sinister and low. "Over there," I whispered, pointing. Elio unslung the rifle. "Come on."

I moved out into the wet ground, and Elio followed.

The grumblers were scavengers, nearly two meters in height, looking like a cut-and-paste, two-legged hybrid of great ape and Komodo dragon, though—like the Miccail and several other local species—they were probably biologically closer to an Earth marsupial than anything else. They walked upright if stooped over, their clawed front hands pulled close, slinking through the night. They were rarely seen near our settlement, seeming to fear the presence of the noisy humans. Sometimes alone, sometimes running in a small pack, they were also generally quiet—hearing one meant that the creature was close, and that it had found something. Grumblers were thieves and scavengers, snatching the kills of other, smaller predators or pouncing on an unsuspecting animal if it looked tiny and helpless enough. I hated them: they were ugly, cowardly, and mean beasts. They invariably ran if challenged.

If one had crept this close to the compound, then it had spotted something worth the danger to itself. Elio and I ran.

The grumbler was leaning over something in a small hollow, still mewling in its bass voice. Hearing us approach, it stood upright, turning its furred snout toward us and exposing double rows of needled teeth. The twinned tongue that was common in Mictlanian wildlife slithered in the mouth. Straggling fur swung under its chin like dreadlocks. Shorter fur cradled the socket of the central lens—like that of the Miccail—placed high in the forehead. The grumbler glared and cocked its head as if appraising us.

It growled. I couldn't see what it had been crouching over, but the grumbler appeared decidedly irritated at having been disturbed. The long, thin arms sliced the air in our direction, the curved slashing claws on the fingers extended. They looked sharper and longer than I remembered.

"Shoo!" I shouted. "Get out of here!" I waved my arms at it. The few times I'd met grumblers before, that had been enough; they'd skulked away like scolded children.

This one didn't move. It growled again, and it took a step toward us.

"Hey—" Elio said behind me. He fired the rifle into the air once. The percussive report echoed over the marsh, deafening. The grumbler jumped backward, crouching, but it held its ground. It snarled now, and took a step forward. I waved at it again.

"Ana . . ." Elio said warningly.

The grumbler gave him no time to say more.

It leaped toward me.

Improvisation, my great-grandmother Anaïs has often told me, *is not just for musicians*. Of course, Geema Ana usually says that when she's decided to use coarse red thread rather than thin white in the pattern she's weaving. I don't think she had situations like this in mind. Or maybe she did, since she was talking about using the materials at hand for your task. For the first time in my life, I demonstrated that I had that skill: I swung my medical bag.

The heavy leather hit the creature in the side of the head and sent it reeling down into the marsh on all fours. The bag broke open, the strap tearing as the contents tumbled out. Shaking its ugly head, the dreadlocks caked with mud, the grumbler snarled and hissed. It gathered itself to leap again. I doubted that the now-empty bag was going to stop it a second time, and I had the feeling that I'd pretty much exhausted my improvisational repertoire.

Elio fired from his hip, with no time to aim. A jagged line of small scarlet craters appeared on the grumbler's muscular chest, and it shrieked, twisting in midair. The grumbler collapsed on the ground in front of me, still slashing with its claws and snapping.

Elio brought the rifle to his shoulder, aimed carefully between the eyes that glared at him in defiance, and pulled the trigger.

The grumbler twitched once and lay still. Its eyes were still open, staring at death with a decided fury.

"What was *that* all about?" I said. I could hardly hear over the sound of blood pounding in my head.

"I don't know. I've never seen one do that before." Elio still hadn't lowered the rifle, as if he were waiting for the grumbler to move again. His face was paler than usual, with a prominent red flush on the cheeks. I could see something dark huddled on the ground where the grumbler had been.

"Elio! There she is!"

I ran.

Euzhan was unconcious, lying on her back. "Oh, God," Elio whispered. I knew he was staring at the girl's blouse—it was torn, and blood darkened the cloth just above the navel. I knelt beside her and gently pulled up the shirt.

The grumbler's claws had laid Euzhan open. The gash was long and deep, exposing the fatty tissue and tearing into muscles, though thankfully it looked like the abdominal wall was intact. "Damn . . ." I muttered; then, for Elio's benefit: "It looks worse than it is." Euzhan had lost blood; it pooled dark and thick under her, but the wound was seeping rather than pulsing—no arterial loss. I allowed myself a quick sigh of relief: we could get her back to the clinic, then. Still, she'd lost a lot of blood, and the unconsciousness worried me.

I quickly probed the rest of body, checked the limbs, felt under the head. There was a swelling bump on the back of her skull, but other than that and the growler's wound, Euzhan appeared unharmed. As I tucked the girl's blouse back down, her eyes fluttered open. "Anaïs? Elio? I'm awful cold," Euzhan said sleepily. I smiled at her and stroked her cheek.

"I'm sure you are, love. Here, Anaïs has a sweater you can wear until we get you back." Euzhan nodded, then her eyes closed again. "Euzhan," I said quietly but firmly. "Euz, no sleeping now, love. I need you to stay awake and talk to me. Do you understand?"

Long eyelashes lifted slightly. Her breath deepened. "Am I going to die, Ana?"

I could barely answer through the sudden constriction in

my throat. "No, honey. You're not going to die. I promise. You lay there very still now, and keep those pretty eyes open. I need to talk to your *da* a second."

"I think we found her in time," I told Elio, covering Euzhan in my sweater. "But we need to move quickly. We have to get her back to the clinic where I can work on her. What I've got in the kit isn't going to do it. Go get us some help. We'll need a stretcher."

Elio didn't move. He stood there, staring down at Euzhan, his eyes wide with worry and fear. I prodded him. "I need you to go now, El. Don't worry—she'll be fine."

That shook him out of his stasis. Elio nodded and broke into a run, calling back to the settlement as he ran.

She'll be fine, I'd promised him.

I hoped I was going to be right.

CONTEXT:
Faika Koda-Shimmura

"THEY FOUND EUZHAN, GEEMA TOZO." FAIKA WAS still breathing hard from the exertion of climbing the stairs to Geema's loft in the tower. Faika, who'd been part of those searching near the old landing pad, had been with the group that helped bring Euzhan back to the Rock. She was still buzzing from the excitement.

Tozo lifted her head from the fragrant incense burning in an ornate holder set on top of a small Miccail stele Tozo used as an altar, but she didn't turn toward Faika. She kept her hands folded together in meditation, her breathing calm and centered, a distinct contrast to Faika's gasping. Several polished stones were set around the base of the stele. Tozo reached out and touched them, each in turn. "I know," she said. "I felt it. She's hurt but alive."

Geema Tozo's tone indicated that her words were more statement than question. But then Tozo always said that she actually talked with the *kami* that lived around the Rock. There were others who were devout, but Tozo lived *Njia*— The Way—as no one else did; at least it seemed so to Faika's somewhat prejudiced eyes. Faika was sure that when the current Kiria, Tami, chose a replacement this coming LastDay, Tozo would be the next Kiria. Faika was a little disappointed that her news wasn't quite the bombshell she'd hoped, but she was also proud that her Geema could know it, just from listening to the voices in her head.

"They took her to the clinic?" Tozo asked. She turned finally. Her face was a network of fine wrinkles, like a piece of paper folded over and over, and the eyes were the brown of nuts in the late fall. Both her hands (and her feet, as Faika knew from seeing Tozo in the Baths) were webbed with a thin sheath of pink skin between the fingers, and the lower half of her face was squeezed together in a faint suggestion of a snout. Faika thought Tozo looked like some ancient and beautiful aquatic animal.

"*Hai*," Faika answered. "Anaïs and Elio found her, and Anaïs was taking care of her. There was a lot of blood. A grumbler—"

"I know," Geema Tozo said, and Faika nodded. The incense hissed and sputtered behind Tozo, and she closed her eyes briefly. "There's trouble coming, Faika. I can feel it. The *kami*, the old ones, are stirring. Anaïs . . ." Tozo sighed.

"Come help me up, child," she said to Faika, extending her hand. "Let's go downstairs. I can smell Giosha's dinner even through the incense, and my stomach's rumbling. What's done is done, and we can't change it."

INTERLUDE:
KaiSa

KAISA STOOD ON THE BLUFF THAT OVERLOOKED THE sea. As Kai expected, BieTe was there: the Old-Father for the local settlement. He was squatting in front of the *nasituda*, the Telling Stone. In one hand he held a bronze drill, in the other was the chipped bulk of his favorite hammerstone. The salt-laden wind ruffled his hair. The sound of his carving was loud in the morning stillness, each note brilliant and distinct against the rhythmic background of surf, separated by a moment of aching silence and anticipation: *T-ching. T-ching. T-ching.* Bie was wearing his ceremonial red robes: the *shangaa.* Flakes of the translucent pale crystal of the stone had settled in his lap, like spring petals on a field of blood.

Bie must have heard Kai's approach, but he gave no sign. KaiSa sniffed the air, fragrant with brine and crisp with the promise of new snow, and opened ker mouth wide to taste all the glorious scents. "The wind is calling the new season, OldFather," ke said. "Can't you hear it?"

Bie grimaced. He snorted once and bared the hard-ridged gums of his mouth in a wide negative without turning around. *T-ching. T-ching.* "I hear—" *T-ching.* "—nothing."

Bie put down the hammerstone. He blew across the carving so that milky rock powder curled into the breeze and away. He stood, lifted his *shangaa* above the hips and carefully urinated on the column. Afterward, he wiped away the excess with the robe's hem to join the multitude of other stains there, a ceremonial three strokes of the cloth: for earth, for air, for water. Where Bie's urine had splashed onto the newly-carved surface, the almost colorless rock slowly darkened to a vivid yellow-orange, highlighting the new figures and matching the other carvings on the stele, while the weathered, oxidized surface of the Telling Stone remained frosty white. Kai could read the hieroglyphic, pictorial writing: the glyph of the OldFather, the wavy line that indicated birth, the glyph of other-self, the slash that made the second figure a diminutive, and the dark circle of femininity.

I, BieTe, declare here that a new female child has been born.

"I decided to take a walk after the birth," Kai said. "Has MasTa named the child?"

"I've not heard her name. Mas said that VeiSaTi hasn't spoken it yet."

Where there should have been joy, there was instead a hue of sullenness in Bie's voice, and Kai knew that ke was the cause of it. Kai nodded. "Mas will give the child strength." Then, because ke knew that it would prick the aloofness that Bie had gathered around himself, ke added: "Mas is a delight, very beautiful and very wise. We're both lucky to enjoy her love."

Kai could see Bie's throat pulse at that. "I know what you're thinking," Bie said. "I know why you came to find me. You're telling me you want to go." Bie's gaze, as brown as the stones of the sea-bluff, drifted away from Kai down to the surging waves, then back. "But I don't want you to leave."

Kai knew this was coming, though ke had hoped that this time it would be different, that for once ker love and affection might emerge unmarred and free of the memory of anger or violence. But—as with most times before—ker wish would not be granted. Kai's mentor JaqSaTu had warned ker of this years ago, when Kai was still bright with the optimism of the newly initiated.

Jaq handed Kai a paglanut and closed ker fingers around the thin, chitinous shell. "Each time, you will think your hands have been filled with joy, but you will be wrong." Jaq told ker. Ke increased the pressure on Kai's fingers, until the ripe nut had broken open. The scent of corruption filled Kai's nostrils—all but one small kernel of the nut was rotten. Jaq plucked the good kernel from the mess in Kai's hand and held it in front of ker. "You will learn to find the nourishment among the rot, or you will starve."

Kai looked at the weathered, handsome face of Bie Old-Father, at the creased, folded lines ke had caressed and licked in the heat of lovemaking, and ke saw that Bie's love had hardened and grown brittle.

"I'm only a servant of VeiSaTi," Kai answered softly and hopelessly. "BieTe, please, you don't want to anger a god. I love you. My time here has been wonderful and for that I wish I could stay, but I have my duty." Kai indicated ker own *shangaa*, dyed bright yellow from the juices of pagla root: VeiSaTi's favored plant, that the god had spewed upon the earth so that all could eat. "Mas has her child. HajXa and CerXa will deliver soon. I have given your people all that a Sa can."

A cloud, driven fast by the high wind, cloaked the sun for a moment before passing. The *brais*, the Sun's Eye high on their foreheads, registered the quick shift in light and both of them crouched instinctively as if ready to flee from a diving wingclaw. Kai watched the scudding clouds pass overhead for a few seconds, then glanced back at Bie. His face was as hard as the Telling Stone, as unyielding as the bronze drill he'd used to carve it. "You should not leave yet," he said. "Tonight, we will give thanks to VeiSaTi for the new child. You must be here for the ceremony."

"And then I may go?"

BieTe didn't answer. He was staring at the Telling Stone, and whatever he was thinking was hidden. He picked up the hammerstone from the ground and hefted it in his hand. "You'll walk back with me now," he said.

There didn't seem to be an answer to that.

BieTe left Kai almost as soon as they reached the village, going off to examine the pagla fields. His mood had not improved during their walk, and Kai was glad to be left alone. Ke went into the TaTe dwelling. "MasTa?" ke called softly.

"In here, Kai."

Kai slid behind the curtain that screened the sleeping quarters. "I'm so happy for you," ke said. "May . . . may I see?"

MasTa smiled at Kai. Almost shyly, she unfastened the closures of her *shangaa*, exposing her body. Sliding a hand down her abdomen, she opened the muscular lip of her youngpouch and let Kai peer inside. The infant, eyes still closed and entirely hairless, not much longer than Kai's hand, was curled at the bottom of the snug pocket of Mas's flesh. Her mouth was fastened on one of Mas's nipples, and her sides heaved in the rapid breath of the newborn as she suckled. "She's beautiful, isn't she?" Mas whispered.

Kai reached into the warm youngpouch and stroked the child gently, enjoying the shiver ker daughter gave as ke touched her. "Yes," ke sighed. "She's beautiful, yes." Reluctantly, ke took ker hand from the pouch and stroked Mas's cheek with fingers still fragrant and moist from the infant. Ke fondled the tight, red-gold curls down her neck. "After all, she's yours."

Mas laughed at that. She let the youngpouch close, fastened her *shangaa* again, and reclined on the pillows supporting her back.

"Tired?" Kai asked.

"A little."

"Then rest. I'll leave you alone to sleep."

"No, Kai," Mas said. "Please."

"All right." Kai settled back into the nest of pillows piled in the sleeping room. For what seemed a long time, ke simply watched Mas, enjoying the way the sunlight burned in her hair and burnished the pattern of her skin as it came through the open window of the residence. As ke gazed at her, ke could feel that part of ker did indeed want to stay, to watch this child of kers and Mas and Bie grow, to see her weaned from the pouch when the weather turned warm again, to listen to her first words and watch the reflection of kerself in the new child's eyes. Mas must have guessed what ke was thinking, for she spoke from her repose, her eyes closed against the sun.

"I know that you must leave. I understand."

"I'm glad someone does." Kai said it as unharshly as ke could.

Her large eyes opened, that surprising flecked blue-green that was so rare and so striking. A knitted covering tied around her head shielded her *brais* from the afternoon glare. "Bei loves you as much as I do. Maybe more. He told me once that you have made him feel whole. He's afraid, Kai. That's all. He's afraid that when you leave, you'll take part of him with you."

"I'm leaving behind far more of myself than I'm taking," Kai answered. Ke stroked ker own belly for emphasis. "I'm leaving behind your child, and Haj and Cer's. I've given you VieSaTi's gift. Now I must give it to others."

"Why?" Mas asked. Her bright, colorful eyes searched ker face.

"Now you sound like BieTe," Kai said, and softened ker words with a laugh. "I'm a Sa. I've been taught the ways of the Sa. After I leave, other Sa will come here."

"And if they don't?"

"You'll still have children," Kai said, answering the question ke knew was hidden behind her words. "With BieTe alone."

"I had three other children before you came," Mas said. "Only one lived, a male. Bie sent him away." Mas averted her eyes, not looking at Kai, and her skin went pale with sadness. Kai's own brown arms whitened in sympathy. "The others . . . well, my first one lived only a season. The other, a female, was wild and strange. She never learned to talk, and she was fey. She would attack me when I was sleeping, or kill the little meatfurs just to watch them die. A wingclaw took her finally, or that's what BieTe told me. I . . . I found it hard to mourn."

"Mas—" Kai leaned forward to hold Mas, but she bared her gums.

"Don't," Mas said. "Don't, because you'll only make me miss you more. You'll only make it harder." Mas brought her legs up. Arms around knees, she hugged herself, as if she was cold. "The sun's almost down. Bie will be starting the ceremony soon. I need to sleep, so I'll be ready."

"I understand," Kai said. . . . *the smell of the rotten paglanut, breaking in ker hand* . . . "I understand. I . . . I'll see you then."

28

Reaching forward, ke patted the youngpouch through her *shangaa*. "Sleep for a bit. Rest." Ke rose and went to the door of the chamber. Stopping there, ke looked back at her, at the way she watched ker.

"I love you, MasTa," ke said.

She didn't smile. "I love you also," she said. "But I wish I didn't."

VOICE:

Anaïs Koda-Levin the Younger

"CLEAN EUZHAN UP AND GET HER INTO A BED," I told our assistants. "She should be waking up in about ten minutes or so—let Hui or me know if she isn't responding. Hayat, we're going to need more whole blood, so after you get Euzhan comfortable, round up three or four of her mi, da, or sibs and get some. Ama, if you'd take charge of the cleanup...."

As they rolled Euzhan away to one of the clinic rooms, I went to the sink and scrubbed the blood and thorn-vine sap from my hands. Hui shuffled alongside me, using the other spigot. When I'd finished drying, I leaned back against the cool wall, frowning through the weariness. Hui shook water from his hands, toweled dry, and tossed the towel in the hamper as I watched his slow, deliberate motions.

I knew what he was going to say before he said it. We'd been working together for that long.

"You did what you could, Anaïs. Now we wait and see." Hui stretched out one ancient forefinger and tapped me gently under the chin. "We can't do anything else for her right now."

"Hui, you saw how close that was." I shivered at the memory. "The descending oblique was nearly severed. If those claws had dug in a few millimeters deeper . . ."

"But they didn't, and Euzhan will fight off infections or she won't, and we'll do what we need to do, whatever happens. Ana, what did I tell you when you first started studying with me?"

That finally coaxed a wan, grudging smile through the fog of exhaustion. "Let's see . . . 'Is that expression normal for you, child, or does catatonia run in your family?' Or how about: 'I'm afraid to let you handle a broom, much less a scalpel.' Oh, and I couldn't forget: 'I'm sure you have *some* qualities, or they wouldn't have sent you to me. Let's hope we manage to stumble across them before you kill someone.' " I shrugged. "Those were some of the milder quotes that I can recall. I was sure you were going to send me home and tell my family that I was hopeless."

Hui snorted. The wrinkles around his almond eyes pressed deeper as he grinned. "I very nearly did. You have a good memory, Anaïs, but a selective one. You've forgotten the one important thing."

"And what was that?"

I could see myself in his dark eyes. I could also see the filmy white of the cataracts that were slowly and irrevocably destroying his vision. Not that Hui would ever complain or even admit it, though I'd noticed—silently—that he'd passed nearly all the surgery to me in the past year. "I once told you that no matter how good you were, you are only a tool in the hands of whatever *kami* inhabits this place. You're a very good tool, Anaïs, and you have done all the work that you're capable of doing for the moment. Be satisfied. Besides, it's no longer you that I'm hounding; it's Hayat and Ama." His forefinger tucked me under my chin once more. "Come on, child."

"I'm not a child, Hui."

"No, you're not. But I still get to call you that. Come on. Dominic will be going apoplectic by now, and we can't afford that at his age."

Hui was right about that. As we came through the doors into the clinic's waiting room, half of the Allen-Shimmura family surged forward toward us, with patriarch Dominic at the fore. I avoided him and tried to give a reassuring smile to Andrea and Hizo, Ochiba's other two children, both of them standing close behind the bulwark of Dominic.

"Well?" the old man snapped. He was as thin as a thornvine stalk, and as prickly. His narrow lips were surrounded by furrows, his black, almost pupilless eyes were overhung by folds. His voice had gone wavery with his great age, but was no less edged for that. The grandson of Rebecca Allen, he was one of the few people left of the third generation. My Geema Anaïs once described Dominic as being like a strip of preserved meat: too salty and dry to decay, and too tough to be worth chewing. "How is she?"

I noticed immediately that Dominic was looking at Hui rather than me, even though the patriarch was aware that I had been in charge of the surgery.

Hui noticed it as well. He had on what I thought of as his "go ahead and make your mistake" face, the expressionless and noncommittal mask he wore when one of his students would look up quizzically while making an incision. Hui leaned against the wall and folded his arms over his chest. "Anaïs did the surgery. All I did was assist." He said nothing more. The silence stretched for several seconds before Dominic finally sniffed, glared at Hui angrily, and turned his sour gaze on me.

"Well?" he snapped once more.

"Euzhan's fine for the moment." I found it easier, after the first few words, to put my regard elsewhere. I let my gaze wander, making eye contact with Euzhan's *mi* and *da*, and favoring Elio with a transient smile. "We cleaned up the wound—nothing vital was injured, but we had to repair more muscle damage than I like. She's going to need therapy afterward, but we'll work out some schedule for that later. Actually, she should be waking up in a few minutes. She's going to be groggy and in some pain—Hui's already prepared painkillers for her. Dominic, I'll leave it to you. It would be good if there were some familiar faces around her when she comes out of the anesthetic. But no more than two of you, please."

Dominic's grim expression relaxed slightly. He allowed her a fleeting, brief half-smile. "Stefani, come with me. Ka-Wai, take the rest of the Family home and get them fed. Tell Bui that he's been damned lucky. Damned lucky." With those abrupt commands, he left the room with his shuffling, slow walk that still somehow managed to appear regal. The rest of the family murmured for a few minutes, thanking me and Hui, and then drifted from the clinic into the cold night. Eventually, only Hui and myself were left.

"He really doesn't like you, does he?"

That garnered a laugh that might have come from the eastern desert. "You noticed."

"So what's the problem between the two of you?"

"What do you *think* is the problem?" I answered shortly, hating the bitterness in my voice but unable to keep the emotion out. "He knows about me, just like you do. 'Poor Anaïs—from what I've heard, there's no chance *she's* going to have children. And what about her and Ochiba? Don't you think they were just a little too *close* . . . ' "

I stopped. Blinked. I was staring at the wall behind Hui, at the pencil and charcoal sketch of Ochiba I'd done years before, while she was pregnant with Euz. Hui had taken the piece without my knowledge from the desk drawer into which I'd stuffed it. He'd matted and framed the drawing, then placed it on the clinic wall as a Naming Day gift. *Don't ever be timid about your talents,* he'd said. *Gifts like yours are too rare on this world to be hidden. And don't hide your feelings, either, girl—those are also far too rare.*

Well, Hui, that's a wonderfully idealistic statement, but it doesn't fit into this world we've made for ourselves. There are some things that are better left stuffed in the drawer.

"You can't let him intimidate you," Hui said. "I don't care how old and venerated he is . . ."

"That's *khudda,* Hui, and we both know it. What Dominic says, goes—and that's true even for the other Families, too. With the exception of Vladimir Allen-Levin and Tozo Koda-Shimmura, Dominic's the Eldest, and poor Vlad's so senile—" I cut off my own words with a motion of my hands. "Hui, we don't need to talk about this. Not now. It's really not important. Euzhan should be coming around about now. Why don't you go back and check on her? Dominic would be more comfortable if you were there."

He didn't protest, which surprised me. Hui touched my shoulder gently, pressing once, then turned. I sat in one of the ornate clinic chairs (carved by my *da* Derek when Hui had declared me "graduated" from his tutelage) and leaned my head back, closing my eyes. I stayed there for several minutes until I heard Dominic and Hui's voices, sounding as if they were heading back into the lobby. I didn't feel like another round of frigid exchanges with Dominic, so I rose and walked into the coldroom lab.

It was warmer there than in his presence.

I set the pot of thorn-vine sap over the bunsen to heat, put on a clean gown and mask, then scrubbed my hands. I plunged still-wet hands into the warm, syrupy goo, then raised them so that the brown-gold, viscous liquid coated my fingers and hands, turning my hands until the sap covered the skin evenly. After it dried, I pulled out the gurney holding the Miccail body. I stared at it (*him? her?*) for a time, not really wanting to work but feeling a need to do something. I straightened the legs, examining again the odd, inexplicable genitalia.

"Ana?"

The voice sent quick shivers through me. I felt my cheeks flush, almost guiltily, and I turned. "El. *Komban wa*. I thought you'd left."

"Went out to get some air." Elio stepped into the room. "I, ummm, just wanted to thank you. For Euzhan. Dominic, he . . . he should have told you himself, but I know that he's grateful, too."

"He didn't need to thank me. Besides, Euzhan's rather special to me, too."

"I know. But Dominic still shouldn't have been so rude." Not many in his Family dared to criticize Dominic to anyone else; the fact that Elio did dampened some of my irritation with him. Elio tugged at the jacket he wore, pulling down the cloth sleeves. "So that's your bogman, huh? Elena told me about how she found it. Pretty ugly."

"Give the poor Miccail a break. You'd be ugly too if you sat in a peat bog for a couple thousand years. It's hell on the complexion."

Elio grinned at that. "Yeah, I guess so. Might give me some color, though. Couldn't hurt." He leaned forward for a closer look, and I felt myself interposing between Elio and the Miccail, as I had earlier. Elio didn't seem to notice. After another glance at the body, he moved away.

"You planning to become the next Gabriela?" he asked, then blushed, as he realized that he'd given the words an undercurrent he hadn't intended. "I mean, you work too much, Ana," he said quickly. "You're always here. When's the last time you did a drawing or went to a Gather?"

Ages. The answer surfaced in my mind. *Far too long.*

But I couldn't say any of the words. I only shrugged. "Elio, if I'm going to get anything done . . ."

"Sorry," he said reflexively. "I understand."

He didn't leave. He watched as I worked patiently on the hand I'd uncovered earlier, straightening the fingers and the ragged webbing between them. When, some time later, he cleared his throat, I looked up.

"Listen," Elio said. "When you're done here, do you have plans? I thought, well, we haven't been together in a long time . . ."

Two years. I haven't been with anyone in almost two years. "El . . ." The unexpected proposition sent guilty thoughts

33

skittering through my mind. *You're the last of the Koda-Levin line, unless Mam Shawna gets pregnant again—and she's already showing signs of menopause. If they heard that you turned someone down, after all this time. . . .*

And then: *Ochiba would tell you to do it. You know she would.*

"El, I just don't know."

"Think about it," he said. Muscles relaxed in his pale face; he gave a faint smile. "It's not because of today," he told me. "Just in case that's what you're thinking."

It had been, of course. Anaïs: the charity fuck. "No. Of course not."

"That's good. It's just that I haven't seen you much recently with all your work, and being with you today, even under the circumstances, I'd forgotten how much I enjoyed talking with you."

I wondered whether he'd also forgotten the miserable failure the last time we tried to make love.

"I'm sorry, Ana. I don't know what the problem is," he said, even though we both knew well enough. I kissed away the apology, pretending that I didn't care. I think I even managed to smile.

I was fairly certain he'd only asked me as a favor to Ochiba.

"No," I said. "It's me. Not you. It's fine. Don't worry about it." But we both had, and Elio had slipped away from my bed as quickly as he could, pleading an early morning appointment we both knew was a fiction.

I had spent the rest of the night alternating between tears and anger.

"Elio, I'm afraid tonight . . . well, it wouldn't be good. I'm tired, and I was planning to stay here, just in case Euz needs some help." I lifted my sap-stained fingers. "I was hoping to get some of this work done, also." The excuses came too fast and probably one too many; I saw in his face that he realized it too. Guilt warred with anxiety over the battle-ground of conscience and won an entirely Pyrrhic victory.

"El, I'm sorry. It's just that I. . . ." I stopped, deciding that there wasn't much use in trying to explain what I didn't fully understand myself. And there was the guilt of turning down an opportunity when I'd yet to become pregnant and those chances seemed to come less and less. "Anyway, I can do this some other time, and chances are Euz is going to be fine. Give me a bit, just to make sure that Euz is stabilized and to clean up again . . ."

I wasn't sure what it was I saw in his face. "Sure. Good. I'll come by then. At your Family compound?"

I nodded. We were being so polite now. "I'll meet you in the common room."

"Okay. See you then." Awkwardly, he leaned over and kissed me. His lips were dry, the touch almost brotherly, but I enjoyed it. Before I could pull his head down to me again, he straightened. Cold air replaced his warmth. "See you about NinthHour?"

"That would be fine."

After Elio had left, I halfheartedly cleaned some of the clinging peat from the folds of the Miccail's face. "What were you like?" I asked the misshapen, crushed flesh. "And do you have any advice for someone who isn't sure she just made the right decision?"

The ancient body didn't answer. I sighed and went to the sink to scrub my hands.

CONTEXT:
Ama Martinez-Santos

THERE WERE TIMES THAT AMA REGRETTED HAVING been apprenticed to Hui. However, Geema Kyra had given her no choice in the matter, and an elder's word was always law. Hui was never satisfied—no matter how fast Ama moved or how well she did something, Hui always pointed out how she could have done it faster, better, or more effectively another way. Hayat was given the same harsh treatment, but that didn't lessen the impact. Ama was fairly certain that it was not possible to satisfy Hui.

And then there was Anaïs. She was just fucking weird. A good doctor, yes, and at least she'd give out a crumb of praise now and then, but she was . . . strange. The way she used all her free time lately examining that nasty body Elena had found. . . .

Anaïs had told her to put the Miccail's body back in the coldroom. Ama threw a sheet over the thing before she moved it—she couldn't stand to see the empty bag of alien flesh; she hated the earthy smell of the creature and the leathery, unnatural feel of its skin. The thing was creepy—

it didn't surprise Ama that it had been killed.

Ama had heard her *mi* and *da* talking—there was a nasty rumor that Anaïs and Ochiba had been lovers, though as Thandi always pointed out, Ochiba had died after giving birth to Euzhan, so if Anaïs was a *rezu*, then it hadn't stopped Ochiba from sleeping with men. Ama sometimes wondered what it would be like, making love to another woman. . . .

She shivered. That was a sure way to be shunned. That's what had happened to Gabriela—the second and final time she had been shunned.

Ama wheeled the gurney into the coldroom. She slid the bog body into its niche and hurried out of the room.

She didn't look back as she turned out the lights. Afterward, she scrubbed her hands at the sink in the autopsy room, twice, even though she knew that would make her late changing Euzhan's dressings and Hui would yell at her again.

VOICE:
Anaïs Koda-Levin the Younger

MOST OF MY EROTIC MEMORIES DON'T INVOLVE fucking. I suppose the wet piston mechanics of sex never aroused me as much as other things. Smaller things. More intimate things.

I can close my eyes and remember . . .

. . . at one of the Gathers, dancing the whirlwind with a few dozen others out on the old shuttle landing pad, when I noticed Marshall Koda-Schmidt watching from the side in front of the bonfire. I was twelve and just a half year past my menarche, which had come much later than I'd wanted. Marsh was older, much older—one of the fifth generation—and in my eyes appeared to be far more sensual than the gawky boys my own age. He stood there, trying to keep up a conversation with Hui over the racing, furious beat of the musicians. I kept watching him as I danced, laughing as I turned and pranced through the intricate steps, and I noticed we both had the same stone on our necklaces. I thought that an omen. During one of the partner changes, there was suddenly an open space between us, and Marsh looked up from his conversation out to the dance. His gaze snared mine; he smiled. At that moment, one of the logs fell and the bonfire erupted into a coiling, writhing column of bright fireflies behind him. I was caught in those eyes, those older and, I thought, wiser eyes. I couldn't take my eyes off him, and every time I looked, it seemed he was also watching me. I smiled; he laughed and applauded me. I felt flushed and giddy, and I laughed louder and danced harder, sweating with the energy even in the night cold, stealing glances toward Marshall. We smiled together, and as I danced, I felt I was dancing with him. For him. To him . . .

. . . Chi-Wa's fingers stroking my bare shoulder and running down my arm, my skin almost electric under his gentle touch, inhaling his warm, sweet breath as we lay there with our mouths open, so close, so close but not quite touching. When his hand had traversed the slope of my arm and slipped off to tumble into the nest of my lap, our lips finally met at the same time . . .

. . . sitting with Ochiba at the preparation table in the Allen-Shimmura compound's huge kitchen, peeling sweetmelon for the dessert. We were just talking, not saying anything important really, but the words didn't matter. I was intoxicated by the sound of Ochiba's voice, drunk on her laugh and the smell of her hair and the sheer familiar presence of her. I'd just finished cutting up one of the melons and Ochiba reached across me to steal a piece. She sucked the fruit into her mouth in exaggerated mock triumph while the orange-red juice ran down her chin in twin streaks. For some reason, that struck us both as hilarious, and we burst into helpless laughter. Ochiba reached over and we hugged, and I was so aware of her body, of the feel of her against me, of how soft her breasts seemed under the faux-cotton blouse. Then the confusion hit, making me blush as I realized that what I was feeling was something I wasn't prepared or expecting to feel, and knowing by the way Ochiba's embrace suddenly tightened around me that she was feeling it as well, and was just as frightened and awed by the emotions as I was . . .

Moments. Those fleeting seconds when the sexual tension is highest, when you're alone in a universe of two where nothing else can intrude.

Of course, then reality usually hits. After the Gather, I

turned down two other offers of company and went back to my compound alone, with one last smile for Marshall. I left my outer door open, certain that Marshall would come to me that night, but he never did.

Chi-Wa was so involved in his own arousal and pleasure that I quickly realized that I was nothing more than another anonymous vessel for his glorious seed.

And Ochiba, the only one of them who was truly important to me . . . well, in another year she was dead.

Tonight, I was keeping reality away with a glass of *da* Joel's pale ale, and trying to stop thinking that it was late and that I wished I'd just told Elio no. There was no one else in the common room; Ché, Joel, and Derek had all grinned, made quick excuses, and left when I'd mentioned that I was staying up because Elio was coming over. I requested the room to play me Gabriela's *Reflections on the Miccail* and leaned back in the chair as the first pulsing chords of the dobra sounded. The chair was one of *da* Jason's creations, with a padded, luxurious curved back that seemed to wrap and enfold you—very womblike, very private: I'd never known Jason, who had died when I was very young, but his was my favorite listening chair. The family pet, a verrechat Derek had rescued from a spring flood five years before, came up and curled into my lap. I stroked the velvety, nearly transparent skin of the creature, and watched its heart pulse behind the glassy muscles and porcelain ribs. I shut my eyes and let the rising drone of the music carry me somewhere else. I barely heard the clock chiming NinthHour.

"I never thought Gabriela was much of a composer."

"She'd have agreed with you," I answered. "And I think you're both wrong. She was a fine composer; the problem was that she just wasn't much of a musician. You have to imagine what she was trying to play rather than what actually came out. Hello, Elio."

I told the room to lower the music and pulled the chair back up. The verrechat glared at me in annoyance and went off in search of a more stable resting place. Elio gave me an uncertain smile. "You looked so comfortable, I almost didn't want to interrupt."

"Sorry. Music's my meditation. I spend more time here than's good for me."

He nodded. I nodded back. Great conversationalists, both of us. I should have kept the music up. At least we could have both pretended to be listening to it. "Any change in

Euzhan?" he asked at last, just as the silence was threatening to swallow us. I hurried into the opening, grateful.

"When I left, she was sleeping. Hui's keeping her doped up right now. When I left, Dominic was still there, but Hui was trying to convince him that camping out in the clinic wasn't going to help. I'm not sure he was making much progress."

"Geeda Dominic can be pretty strong-willed."

"Uh-huh. And water can be pretty wet."

Elio grinned. The grin faded slowly, and he was just Elio again. We both looked at each other. "Ummm," he began.

If you're going through with this, then do it, I told myself. "Elio, let's go to my room," I said, trying to make it sound like something other than "And get this over with." I was rewarded with a faint smile, so maybe Elio wasn't as reluctant as I'd thought. I'd been planning to let him back out now, if that's what he wanted, figuring that if this *was* simply a guilt fuck, we were both better off without it—for most women I knew, sex simply for the sake of sex was something you did the first year or two after menarche. By then, you'd gone through most of the available or interested males on Mictlan. In my case, that hadn't been too many, not after the first time around. Since then, with one glorious and forbidden exception, the only regular liason I've had has been with Hui's speculum and some cold semen, once a month.

Even that hasn't worked out.

All that was long ago. Forget it. The voice wasn't entirely convincing, but I held out my hand, and Elio took the invitation without hesitating. Tugging on my fingers, he pulled me toward him, and this time he kissed me. There was a hunger in the kiss this time, and I found parts of me awakening that I thought had been dead.

I suddenly wanted this to work, and that increased my nervousness. I wondered if he could tell how scared I was.

Elio either sensed that fright, or he'd learned a lot since the last time. In my admittedly noncomprehensive experience, men tended to go straight for the kill, shedding clothes on the way so they didn't snag them on rampant erections. Maybe that was just youthful exuberance, but I'd spent many postcoital hours crying, believing that the quickness and remoteness was because they wanted to get the deed done as fast as possible. Because it was *me*. 'Just doing my duty, ma'am. Have to make sure that we increase the population, after all. Nothing personal.'

Except that sex is always personal and always intimate, no matter what the reasons for it might be. In the midst, I might look up to see my partner's eyes closed, a look almost of pain on his face as he thrust into me, and I knew he was gone, lost in imagined couplings with someone else.

Not *with* me. Never *with* me. Never together.

Elio pulled away. I breathed, watching him. He was still here. "This way," I said, and led him off.

I'd done some quick housekeeping before he'd come, and the room actually looked halfway neat except for the mirror, as always draped in clothing. Through the folds I caught a reflection of someone who looked like me, her face twisted in uncertain lines.

When I closed the door and turned, Elio was closer to me than I expected, and I started, leaning back against the jamb. He touched my cheek, stroked my hair. As his hand cupped the back of my head, he pulled me into him, his arms going around me. Neither of us had said anything. I leaned my head against his shoulder. He continued to stroke my hair.

I wondered what he was thinking, and when I turned my head up to look, he kissed me again: gently, warmly, his lips slightly parted. This time the kiss was longer, more demanding, and I found myself opening my mouth to him, pulling his head down even further. His hands dropped from my shoulders; his fingers teased my nipples through my blouse, and they responded to his touch, ripening and making me shudder.

When we finally broke apart again, his pale eyes searched mine with soft questions. I reached behind us and touched the wall plate, the lights gliding down into darkness as I did so. "I can't see, Ana."

"You don't need to."

"I'd like to look at you."

"Elio . . ."

A pause. Silence. He waited.

Biting my lower lip, I touched the plate again, letting the lights rise to a golden dimness. I stepped deliberately away from him. Standing in front of my bed, I undid the buttons of my blouse, of my pants. I held the clothes to me, hugging myself, then took a breath and let them fall to the floor. I stood before Elio, defiantly naked. I shivered, though the room wasn't cold.

I knew what he was seeing. I might keep my mirror covered, but I knew.

Under a wide-featured face, he saw a woman's body, with small breasts and flared hips. Extending below the triangle of pubic hair, though, there was something wrong, something that didn't belong: a hint of curved flesh.

An elongated, enlarged clitoris, Hui had told my mother, who noticed it at birth: a paranoid, detailed examination of every newborn child is Mictlan's birthright. *A slight to moderate hermaphrodism. I doubt that it's anything to stop her from reaching her Naming. Everything else is female and normal. She may never notice.*

Maybe Hui would have been right had everything stayed as it was when I was a child. I certainly paid no attention to my small deformity, nor did anyone else. I didn't seem much different from the other little girls I saw. After menarche, though. . . . My periods from the beginning were so slight as to be nearly unnoticeable and the pale spottings weren't at all like the dark menstrual flow of the other women. I also began to notice how sensitive I was there, how the oversized nub of flesh had begun to change, to swell until the growth protruded well past my labial folds, pushing them apart before ducking under the taut and distended clitoral hood.

Over the years, even after menarche, the change continued. The last time I glanced at a mirror, I thought I looked like an effeminate and not particularly pretty young man with his penis tucked between his legs, pretending to be a woman.

Elio's gaze never drifted that low. I noticed, and tried to pretend that it didn't matter. I wanted to believe that it didn't matter. He took a step toward me. He cupped my breasts in his hands, his skin so pale against mine. I fumbled with his shirt, finally getting it open and sliding it down his shoulders. Elio was thin, though his waist rounded gently at the belt line.

His skin was very warm.

I pulled him into bed on top of me.

. . . and sometime later . . .

. . . later . . .

No, I'm sorry. I can't say. I won't say.

JOURNAL ENTRY:
Gabriela Rusack

I WAS A SLOW LEARNER WHEN IT CAME TO THE difference between love and sex. Oh, I knew that people could enjoy sex without being in love with the person they're with at the moment. God knows I experienced that myself often enough ... and often enough kicked myself in the morning for paying attention to whining hormones.

As I grew older, I slowly realized that the reverse was also a possibility—I could be in love with someone and *not* have sex with them, if that wasn't in the cards. I needed friends more than I needed lovers, and I found that sex can actually destroy love.

Lacina was my college roommate, and my friend. At the time, I was still mainly heterosexual, though I'd already had my first tentative encounters with women. I think Lacina suspected that I was experimenting, but we never really talked about it. I dated guys and slept with some of them, just as she did, so if on rare occasions a girlfriend stayed overnight, she just shrugged and said nothing. One Friday night in my junior year, neither of us had a date. We were drinking cheap wine and watching erotic holos in our apartment, and the wine and the holos had made us both silly and horny. I remember putting my arm around Lacina, playfully, and how sweet her lips were when I finally leaned over to kiss her, and her breathy gasp when I touched her breasts. ... We tumbled into my bed and I made love to her, and showed her how to make love to me. But the next morning, when the wine fumes had cleared. ...

After that night, it was never the same between us. There was a wall inside Lacina that had never been there before, and she flinched if I'd come near her or touch her. I don't know why she was retreated. I don't know what old guilt I'd tapped; afterward, it wasn't a subject on which she'd allow discussion. She pretended that our night together had never happened. She pretended that things were the same

42

as they had been, but they weren't, and we both knew it. At the end of the semester, she moved out.

No, sex and love are basically independent of each other. Not that it matters for me, not anymore. My closest friends are dead, and those here on Mictlan that I thought were friends won't talk to me at all anymore.

No more sex. No more love. I spend my remaining days with the only passion I have left, the only passion allowed me: the cold and dead Miccail.

Now if sex, love, and passion are intricate, varied, and dangerous for us, then the sexuality of the Miccail must have been positively labyrinthian. I can only imagine how convoluted their relationships were, with the midmale sex complicating things. I wonder *how* they loved, and I try to decipher the answer from the few clues left: the stelae, the crumbling ruins, the ancient artifacts. I wonder why this world saw fit to add another sex into the biological mix, but the past holds its secrets too well.

What frightens me is that I'm certain it's important for us to know. The Miccail died only a thousand years ago. With all the artifacts, all the structures they left behind, none of them we've found are any younger than that. From what I've been able to determine, the collapse and decline of the Miccail began another thousand years before their extinction, possibly linked with the rapid disappearance of the midmales, all mention of whom vanish from the stelae at that point. One short millennium later—barely a breath in the life of the world and the Miccail's own long history—and the Miccail were gone, every last one.

It's almost as if Something didn't like them.

And now *we're* here, filling our lungs and our bodies with Mictlan-stuff. Yes, we sampled and tested Mictlan's air, water and soil, let it flow through the assorted filters and gauges until the machines stamped the world with their cold imprimatur. The proportion of gases was within our body tolerances. We could taste the winds of this world and live. Our lungs would move, the oxygen would flow in our blood. But Mictlan is not Earth. The atmosphere of a world holds its own life, and life moves within it.

So we take a deep breath of Mictlan and we bring the alien presence into our lungs because we have no choice. We will slowly become Mictlan. Mictlan will become us.

And the Something that obliterated the Miccail will take a

long look at us: because we are here, because we breathe, because we drink the water and eat the plants.

I wonder if that Something will like us better than it did the Miccail.

INTERLUDE:
KaiSa

AFTER LEAVING MASTA, KAI HAD GONE DIRECTLY TO ker rooms in the TeTa house and packed the few belongings which were truly kers into ker traveling pouch: the well-used grinding stones for herbs and potions which JaqSa had given ker as a parting gift the first time ke'd left the sacred Sa island called AnglSaiye; the parchment book of medicines, written in the private language of the Sa with the sacred inks only the Sa knew how to make; the relic of VeiSaTi which was ker authorization to move freely outside the island, and the tools of sacrifice. Ke left behind the fine anklet BieTe had carved for ker from redstone, with crystalline images of BieTe and MasTa's sacred animals set in the swirling, ornate patterns. Keeping the jewelry would only remind ker of Bie and Mas, and of the children ke had helped to sire here.

It was painful enough to leave. It was even more painful to have to remember.

Kai shouldered ker pack and pushed open the door. A hand pushed ker back inside: NosXe, one of BieTe's adopted sons. Kai stumbled and fell backward, striking ker left shoulder hard on the flagstone floor. "My father said you would try to leave," Nos grumbled. "You don't know how much BieTe and MasTa care for you, KaiSa."

"I know all too well, Nos," Kai answered. "And if I didn't love them in return, I wouldn't be leaving now. Cycles from now, if you become Te, you will understand that. Tell me, Nos, did BieTe or MasTa send you here?"

NosXe didn't have to answer; the grim stubbornness on his face told Kai that the young son of Bie had acted on his own. Kai rubbed ker sore shoulder, knowing it would shame Nos even more to see that he had injured a Sa.

"I thought not. Your Ta and Te know that it's the curse of Sa to always travel, to leave those they love most. Your Ta and Te know that no matter how much they would like me to stay, I cannot. And they cannot make me stay, not without raising the wrath of VeiSaTi Kerself. Is that what you're willing to risk, Nos? Are you willing to defy a god?"

Always before, that had worked. It was the threat of VeiSaTi's anger that kept all Sa safe. Kai thought that the warning, a doctrine taught to all of the CieTiLa—The People—from childhood, had worked now. Still rubbing ker shoulder, ke got to ker feet and started to walk out past the grim-faced Nos, who still blocked the doorway. But as ke brushed past, Nos reached out with a hand and grabbed Kai's shoulder with his right hand, his talons slightly extended.

"No," Nos started to say, but Kai had already reacted.

Kai slapped ker left hand on top of Nos's, claws out. At the same time, ke turned ker hip back and brought ker right arm on top of Nos's, dropping ker weight. Cloth tore on Kai's shoulder, but Nos howled in pain as his wrist was torqued. The much larger Xe collapsed to his knees to escape the pressure, and Kai completed the pin, taking the struggling Nos down to the floor. Holding Nos's wrist with one hand, ke reached out with ker long fingers and pressed them on either side of Nos's neck, just below the ears—closing the arteries. Nos's struggles became weaker; a few seconds later, he went limp.

Kai released the pin. Ke checked to make sure that Nos was still breathing, then stood. "The Sa are also taught to protect those they love," Kai told the unconscious Nos. "That is another thing you must learn. What you love most is also the most dangerous to you."

Ke stepped over Nos. Ke found that now that it was over, ke was shaking from the sudden encounter. The settlement of BieTe and MasTa, which had once seemed so peaceful and welcoming, now frightened ker.

Ke walked away, almost at a run.

BieTe had started the ceremonial fire on the bluff overlooking the sea. KaiSa could see the smear of dark smoke against the twilight sky and the silhouetted figures of BieTe's people as they moved in the preliminary dance of welcome to the new infant. But Kai saw them only in the distance.

45

Ke moved quickly from the settlement into the woods. A few of the Je and Ja saw ker, but—under the bonds of servitude and at the bottom of the social structure of the CieTiLa—there was no chance that any of them would, like NosXe, challenge Kai's right to go where ke wanted, whenever ke wanted. One of the Ja watched as ke moved away from the cluster of wood and stone buildings; Kai knew that the word would get to BieTe, either from the Ja or from NosXe, as soon as he returned to the ceremony, but by that time it would be too late.

I'm sorry that it had to be this way, Kai told the distant image of the fire. *BieTe, MasTa, I'm sorry to miss the ceremony for my own daughter, but in your hearts, you understand. You must understand. You know the laws as well as I do. A Sa must give ker Gift to all CieTiLa, and that means I must hurt the two of you.*

It means I must hurt myself.

KaiSa put ker back to the fire, to BieTe and MasTa, and to ker daughters and sons, and moved into the forest.

Under the canopy of sweet-leaves, the twilight quickly shifted to full night. The wind was from the west, shivering the leaves with its chill and bringing the scent of flowers. A wingclaw called from its night roost high in one of the trees, the creature's ululating whoop raising the hairs on Kai's arms. The phosphorescent mosses on the many-trunked trees framed the darkness, and the double moons were up, Chali just setting, though Quali was well above the horizon in the east, bright enough that ke could almost see the colors of the leaves. The sound of ker feet shushing through the fallen leaves seemed the loudest sound, though the rhythmic *kuh-whump* of the slickskins calling for their mates in a nearby pond was a constant backdrop.

It was tempting to stop, to try and listen to the voice of VeiSaTi in the rustling and chirping of the world, but there was no time for that now.

Kai knew that there was a wayhouse not far distant. Until ke had actually made the decision to leave, ke had given no thought to where ke might go next. Now, ke determined to stop for the rest of the night at the wayhouse. Ke lengthened ker stride, falling into ker quick walking pace.

When Quali had reached the zenith, its silver light painting the edges of the leaves, Kai came upon the High Road and the wayhouse. The High Road was the main artery through the CieTiLa lands, a trail of flagged stone, a path between all the settlements of the CieTiLa designed by the legendary Sa leader NasiSaTu over six *terduva* ago, and completed by ker successors after NasiSaTu's sacrificial death. The various segments of the road were maintained by the Te and Ta of the lands in which they passed, part of the payment for the services of the mendicant Sa order.

The *nasituda* set in front of the wayhouse declared it to be on the border of the territory of GaiTe and CiTa. For the first time since ke had left, Kai felt ker muscles relax fully, releasing a tension ke hadn't even known ke'd been holding. A light from an oil lamp glimmered behind the translucent window, made from the *brais* of one of the huge but slow thunderbeasts: someone else was already in the wayhouse. Kai gave a low, warbling call of greeting as ke approached the building, waited the polite sequence of sixteen slow breaths, then entered, brushing aside the thunderbeast hide door covering.

The wayhouse was built along typical CieTiLa lines: a large common room where travelers could talk and eat; a small kitchen to the left for food preparation and storage, and three tiny sleeping cubicles to the right. The privacy curtain was drawn on one of those, and a Sa poked ker head out as Kai entered, rubbing ker eyes sleepily.

"Kai?"

"AbriSa!"

Abri tumbled out of the low sleeping cubicle and ran to Kai. The two Sa embraced, laughing. Kai had come to the island some time after Abri's arrival, and the older youth had been one of Kai's mentors, comforting the disoriented and frightened child of three cycles and helping to teach Kai the intricate structure of Sa life. It was Abri who, when Kai had taken First Vows, had taken an inked needle to Kai's chest and marked ker with the symbol of AnglSaiye. Kai's debt to Abri had been paid long ago, when Kai had kerself taken one of the arriving children as ker special project, passing along the knowledge Abri had given ker. Abri had left the AnglSaiye sanctuary long before Kai had been given JaqSaTu's blessing and ker own sanction to begin ker travels through the CieTiLa lands. Kai held Abri at arm's length, looking at ker. ke could see the cycles and the pain of many separations in ker face, in the flesh-hewn valleys of experience VeiSaTi had etched there.

"Where are you traveling to, Abri?" Kai asked when they finally pulled apart. *Where are you going? Where have you been?* Those were the eternal questions of Sa meeting on the road.

"Actually, I was looking for you, among others."

"For me? You're joking. Why?"

Abri didn't answer. Instead, ke pulled away from Kai, and the furrows in ker face deepened as ke frowned. "Let me fix some *kav*. You looked tired," ke said.

Kai watched Abri as ke went into the kitchen and poured the bittersweet, herbal brew into two wooden mugs. "I've been on the island for the past two cycles," ke said as ke placed the pottery jug back into the coldbox sunk into the kitchen's floor. Ke brought the mugs out and handed one to Kai. Ke sipped carefully—"once for TeTa, again for XeXa, and last for JeJa," three being the sacred number of Vei-SaTi—then sank down onto one of the large pillows at the edge of the eating pit. "There have been disturbing rumors, Kai," ke said finally. "I'm just one of several who have been sent out by JaqSaTu to bring all Sa back to the island."

The words sent the *kav* swirling, almost spilling from the mug as Kai started. *To bring all the Sa back to AnglSaiye, bring all of us back from our journeys. . . .* It was something that had never been done before, in all the cycles upon cycles written down on the *nasitudas* set on AnglSaiye's shores. It was something Kai could very nearly not comprehend. "I don't understand . . ."

"You will, when you get back there." Abri sipped ker *kav* once more, staring into the brown depths of the mug. "I really can't say more, except to say that it is becoming a dangerous world for Sa."

Kai, remembering BieTe and MasTa, and ker departure of only a few hours ago, opened hard-ridged lips in a grin. "Love is always dangerous, AbriSa. I have the bruises to prove it."

But Abri didn't share in the jest. Abri's dark, expressive eyes regarded Kai's, and there was pain in ker gaze.

"This is different, Kai," ke said. "This is something no Sa has faced before."

CONTEXT:
Masafumi Martinez-Santos

MASA GRUNTED AS HE SLUNG THE FISH ONTO THE kitchen's well-used preparation table. The river grouper was a meter long and nearly twenty-five kilos. A steel cable ran through the mouth and out the gill slits, and thin streamers of blood trickled from the flank and dripped from Masa's overalls onto the stone-flagged floor.

Masa leaned his gig and spear against the wall, and pulled the straps of the stiff, sap-impregnated overalls from his shoulders. Stepping out of the legs, he tossed the overalls down the stairwell to the washing rooms. He stood in the kitchen in soggy woolen underclothes.

"I suppose you expect me to clean that," his *mi* Adja said. She was pulling loaves from the oven, and the yeasty smell of warm bread fought the river scent of the grouper. Adja moved stiffly—her spine had fused in early childhood, not allowing her to bend over or to turn without moving her whole body. She turned liked a marionette lashed to hidden strings, using her legs to move up and down.

"I did the hard work. Should've seen it fight. The groupers are running back to the sea early this year. The swarm knocked me down twice before I snagged this one, and you know how fucking cold the river is. The overalls leaked— Luis needs to put more thornvine sap on them. I'm freezing and wet and hungry." He started to reach past Adja to the bread steaming on the counter.

Adja slapped his hand away. The *crack* of her hand on his was surprisingly loud. "There's your dinner, dripping all over my clean floor. You can have *sashimi*, or you can help me gut and fillet the beast."

"Damn it, Adja . . ."

"Damn it yourself, Masa. Just because it's my rotation in the kitchen doesn't mean I do all the work."

"I need to go *out*, Adja."

Adja sniffed. "So who are you seeing now?"

49

Masa grinned. "Whoever wants to see me. I'm not picky."

"So I've heard." Adja removed another tray of loaves from the oven, rotating her whole upper body as she set the bread on the cooling racks. "Masa, you need to be careful. There's talk in the Baths."

"What kind of talk?"

"That you're sometimes rough. That you can hurt. Masa, I've told you—with your past, you can't afford that."

"*Khudda*," Masa said. "Who's saying that crap about me?"

Adja shrugged. "It doesn't matter. I'm just telling you for your own good."

Masa grimaced. "All right, so I'm told. If they don't like me, they don't have to fuck me, do they?"

Adja's face hardened. Her eyes narrowed, the lips pursed. If Masa noticed, he pretended not to care. She opened a drawer and rummaged in it. Steel clashed. She pulled out a filleting knife and laid it alongside the grouper. "Take care of the fish. Then you can do whatever you want to do."

Almost, Masa refused. But that would have led to Adja complaining to his mam Seela, and then Geema Kyra would have gotten involved, and the rest of the Family. Too much trouble. Instead, as he scraped the scales from the grouper and slit open the belly, he pretended that it was one of *them*, one of the women talking about him in the Baths.

The thought gave him an erection that lasted until long afterward.

VOICE:
Elio Allen-Shimmura

DOMINIC WOULDN'T TALK TO ME FOR THREE DAYS after I was with Anaïs, enclosing himself in an atmosphere of cold, silent fury. Whenever he saw me in the compound his eyes narrowed until they looked like Tlilapan: black ponds nearly hidden in the folds holding them. His lips pressed together until they appeared to form more of a sphincter than a mouth, and he would make sure I noticed his glare, which was damn near incandescent.

For my part, I made certain that he noticed that I noticed, and didn't give him the reaction he wanted. I may love Dominic, but I don't *like* him.

A lot of the Family feel that way, even if very few of them will admit it.

At the table at SixthHour, where he always ruled the conversation, I was pointedly not invited to offer my opinion on the subject *de jour*, and when I deigned to do so anyway, there was a quick silence as everyone paid rapt attention to the food on their plates. Not that it mattered—the subject was always Euzhan and her progress. Funny how Dominic managed to avoid mentioning Anaïs's name during those conversations, even though I knew Ana was tending Euz as if she were her own child.

I'm certain that word was judiciously leaked to Dominic from the others in my Family that I spent a night with someone else the night *after* I'd been with Anaïs. It didn't require a hell of a psychological background to figure out the reasons underlying that decision. Even so, I was amazed at the relief I felt when, yes, the equipment still worked, thank you very much.

Finally, on the fourth day, as I was sitting in the common room talking with young Dominic and Sarah a little past FirstHour, Geeda Dominic came into the room. He dismissed Domi and Sarah with a barely perceptible nod of his head; they scattered. Andrea, Bui, and Hizo, noisily playing jackstones in a corner, judiciously decided to continue the game somewhere else.

It was suddenly very quiet in the room. I could hear the soft hissing of the peat brick fire in the stone hearth. I watched Dominic sit—no one else ever dared sit in *that* chair, one of Jason Koda-Levin's intricate creations. The chair was (very quietly) called "the throne" by most of us. Dominic grumbled and muttered to himself until he was comfortable, holding his hands out toward the glowing peat, then took a long, slow inhalation that wobbled the loose skin under his chin. I waited. Finally, he looked at me.

"Well, is it true?"

"Is *what* true, Geeda Dominic?" I knew what he wanted to hear, but I wasn't going to give him the satisfaction.

He snorted. Whatever anyone might think of Dominic, his advanced age hadn't made him senile, at least not in that way. "You're not stupid, Elio, though you are often an ass. I'm too old to enjoy playing games that simply waste time, and I'd appreciate it if you don't indulge in them."

"All the nasty rumors to the contrary, Anaïs is female, Geeda," I told him. "A woman. Pretty damn good in bed, too."

Dominic nearly hissed at that—that was obviously not the answer he wanted. He rose from his chair faster than I'd seen him move in years.

"I don't understand you, Elio," he barked, standing in front of me, leaning heavily on his cane; I could see his hand on the copper-plated knob, with the extra vestigial finger jutting uselessly from the side. "You know what she did to Ochiba."

"Anaïs didn't do anything to Ochiba, Geeda. Ochiba died from complications after childbirth. It's a damned shame, but it happens."

"No!" Dominic spat, as I hit the nerve I'd aimed for. "Ochiba was *killed*, killed because of that . . . that *rezu's* jealousy. Ochiba told me that. She stood in my room and said that Euzhan would be her last pregnancy—all because Anaïs had told her it was 'dangerous.' She said that Anaïs didn't even want her to have this one. Anaïs didn't want Ochiba to have another child so she could have Ochiba for herself. And when Ochiba had a child anyway, the vile woman took the opportunity and killed her."

I'd heard parts of this horrible speculation of Dominic's before, in whispered gossip from the older Family members. He'd begun to voice these suspicions not long after Ochiba's death, and the theory had grown and solidified over the years. This was the first time he'd spoken of it openly to me; the blind anger in his voice was nearly visible. "Geeda, we both know that's not what happened," I said. He didn't listen. He was full into his tirade now, and no mere truth was going to dam the vitrolic flood.

". . . and yet you went to her. I've talked to Diana, who has seen Anaïs in the Baths, even though she tries to hide herself. She's deformed, she'll never have children, and because of her, Ochiba—who gave us four named children and would have given us more—is dead. Dead because she and Anaïs were—" He started to say the word. I saw him form it, and then close his mouth before it could emerge. *Lovers.* "Yet you'd lie for her," he finished.

"She saved Euzhan." *And I like her,* I should have added. *She and Ochiba may have been more than our little society wants to tolerate, but I don't care—I never saw Ochiba happier than she was during those months when she and Anaïs were close. I enjoy Anaïs's company. I think she has a wonderful laugh, on those rare occasions when you can manage to coax one out of her. She works harder than anyone around here, and at least a dozen people we can both name wouldn't be here if Anaïs wasn't the best damned doctor we have. I think she's been hurt enough, and she doesn't deserve the crap you've handed her over the last few years.*

But I didn't say any of that. Dominic wouldn't have listened, anyway.

"*Hui* saved Euzhan," Dominic snapped back, his mouth closing sharply on the last syllable. "Anaïs is a freak, and she's responsible for Ochiba's death. I know it, you know it. She shouldn't be tolerated, or she'll corrupt someone else the way she did Ochiba. We can't afford that. No Family can."

"Geeda, Ochiba was her own woman. Any decisions she made, she made on her own. Anaïs didn't kill Ochiba; Mictlan killed her."

"*Phah!*" Dominic slammed the end of the cane on the floor for emphasis. "I won't stand betrayal, Elio. You remember that, boy. I won't stand it. The time is coming when Families will need to make hard decisions. Hard decisions—do you hear me?"

Dominic left the room with a last glare at me. I heard him snarling like a grumbler at the children in the hallway as he passed. They gave him meek, quick apologies. I sat in the chair assessing my various mental wounds; none of them seemed mortal. I figured I was set for at least another week of the Distant Glares, though.

I did wonder why I'd lied. "*Anaïs is female, Geeda . . .*" Well, honestly, Geeda Dominic, I'm not certain. A few years ago when I was with her, that extra ridge of flesh—like a featureless, thick finger shielding her opening—had confused me. Defeated me. Distracted as I was by it, well, I just *couldn't. . . .* That wasn't Anaïs's fault; it was mine.

This time . . . I still wasn't sure what had happened.

This time, I'd managed to get beyond her deformity, to put it out of my mind. I concentrated on her face, her breasts, her skin, her kiss. And once I was inside her, hell, she didn't feel much different than any other woman I've been with, and we were both responding. I was getting close . . . then I remember her shriek, which I think was more surprise than pain. There was a quick, strange hardness intruding between us, like a cock but smaller. I came at almost the same time.

And so did she. I heard her gasp, and cry out. And then . . .

I rolled away from her, shocked at the sudden sticky wetness all over my stomach, all over hers. As Ana sat up, her eyes frantic, I caught a glimpse of something in the tangle of pubic hair, like a child's uncircumcised cock. There was blood, too, at the tip, as if it had just torn free from wherever it had been attached. The fold of flesh guarding her opening was gone. I said something, I don't really remember what—probably something inane and stupid like "Are you all right?"

She was frantic, but again I think it was more from fear than any pain. Or maybe that's just rationalization, because I didn't go to her. Hell, if something that weird happened to me. . . . Anyway, I stood there, that stuff dripping slowly down my stomach, thicker and more yellow than my come. She kept saying, "What's happening to me . . . ?" over and over, wiping at herself with the sheet and then clutching it to her like a shield. She turned away from me. "Get out, Elio," she said harshly, then more gently: "Please, Elio. Please go."

Her naked back was to me. I could see her shoulders begin to shake with the first tears.

A truly compassionate person would have stayed with her. A person who wanted to be her friend as well as a lover would have stayed, would have shown her some compassion. Half the people in our generation have physical defects of one kind or another, varying from trivial to serious. So this one shouldn't matter—look at the spots on my skin.

"Please go," she told me. "I really want you to go . . ."

. . . and, well, I *went*.

I've tried to figure that one out, and the truth is that for that one moment, I was as disgusted and repelled by what I saw in front of me as Dominic would have been. I felt, I don't know . . .

Dirty. Unclean. Contaminated.

I left. I took a long shower afterward, cleaning myself over and over again, and hating myself for the fact that it mattered.

It wasn't Ana's fault. None of it was her fault—I don't know *what* she is, but she didn't ask to be made that way. I could see that much in her eyes, in the way she acted with me just before. Maybe that's why I lied to Dominic now, trying to make up for past failures. Trying to do penance for some of the guilt.

Too fucking bad I didn't feel particularly absolved.

CONTEXT:
Hui Koda-Schmidt

"SINCE ELIO HAS BEEN SEEING HER, I DEMAND TO know—as eldest of my family, Hui—whether Anaïs is a woman or an abomination."

Hui grimaced. On his desk was a crystalline card. The light from his desk lamp coaxed a three-dimensional, moving image of a smiling oriental woman from the card's surface: Akiko Koda, his ancestor. The card, his mam Melissa had told him, had been her ID card for the *Ibn Battuta*. Melissa had been given the card by her mam, Eleanor, who had been Akiko's daughter.

Lately, the card was Hui's meditation in times of stress. He'd certainly never known Akiko, who had died in the Great Storm of 23. Eleanor had given Hui the card just before her final illness a few years ago. "I look at this sometimes and pretend that she's still there, listening to me, even though I was only a year old when she died," Eleanor had told Hui. "Maybe she'll be there for you, too. I will be. I promise."

Hui wondered if Akiko's *kami* was watching, and what she might think of Mictlan now. Akiko's image turned toward him, slightly blurred through his cataracts, and smiled its eternal smile. Decades ago, Eleanor had told him, the card could speak: Akiko's voice, giving her name. No longer. There was only the silent presence of his great-grandmam.

"Anaïs is a fine doctor, Dominic. That's all you need to know. That's all I'm telling you."

"*Khudda*, Hui." Dominic waved his cane, his six-fingered, knobby-jointed hand clutching the polished knob of wood at the end. "I'm not asking much of you. You know her; you examine her every few months. You know damn well that she and my Ochiba were . . . involved. I want to know. It's my *right* to know."

Dominic's lips were pulled back, the dark eyes squinted, and his head was tilted back arrogantly, his nostrils flared.

55

Outrage Personified. The expression on the ancient face might have made Hui laugh, under other circumstances. Under other circumstances. . . . But this was now, and he found himself rising from his chair and matching the old man stance for stance. Akiko's card clattered on wood as he let it drop.

"You're old, Dominic, and you had the privilege to actually know some of the Founders. That gives you a certain status in this society, and grants you certain privileges, but it grants you no *rights*. At least none that I'll acknowledge. I'm going to tell you this once, then I expect you to leave. Anaïs is a fine person and a fine doctor, and without her, one hell of a lot of people here would not be walking around spreading nasty rumors. Even if Ochiba and Ana were lovers—and I'm saying *if*, Domi—that obviously didn't stop Ochiba from conceiving children, so what does it matter? As to what I've seen in my examinations of Anaïs, that's my business, not yours."

Dominic sniffed. "But if she were normal, you'd say so, wouldn't you? And you won't. You can't."

Hui felt his cheeks coloring. He slapped his hand on the desk. "There are *none* of us 'normal' here, Dominic. None. Not me, not you, not anyone. Now, get out of my office. I'm tired of talking nonsense."

Dominic slammed the end of his cane on the floor with an exasperated *huff*. He glared; Hui glared back. Finally, he turned and walked to the door, but stopped before he left. He spoke without turning around to Hui again. "We live in a fragile society," Dominic said. "As an elder, it's my job to protect us from things that threaten what stability we have. And I *will* protect us, Hui—no matter who it hurts."

Hui had no answer to that. He touched the card, and Akiko's image sprang to life. His ancestor smiled wordlessly at him as the sound of Dominic's cane slowly faded down the corridor.

VOICE:
Elio Allen-Shimmura

THE SNOW WAS ORANGE-RED WITH ALGAE THE storm had picked up from Crookjaw Bay. The world appeared to have rusted. The flakes tasted vaguely sour. Both Masafumi and I looked like we'd been bleeding where the snow had melted.

"Did you really fuck Anaïs?"

I was beginning to wonder if everyone was going to be asking that question, albeit a little more politely. "Yeah," I answered tentatively, the word lifting at the end into almost a question as I squinted into the flake-infested wind. "I did."

Masafumi raised thick eyebrows at that. He hefted the rifle he was carrying and flicked some clinging snow from the barrel. "I heard that old Dominic was mightily pissed."

I frowned. "Who told you that?"

"Your sib Sarah." Masa paused and gave me a grin I wished I could give back. "I was with her last night."

Masafumi Martinez-Santos looks like something hewn from a block of wood rather than born. Everything about him is thick and rough: the ledges above his eyes, his cheekbones, his chin, his hands. His skin is dry and scaly, as if some ancient reptilian ancestor infested the coils of his DNA. Bundled up as he was now, he looked like a troll.

Too bad there wasn't any damn sun.

"Sarah should keep her mouth shut." *And her legs.* I thought nastily. Sarah rarely turns down any offer of sex. Of course, she also has four named children, and at 29, is angling for another. Still, *Masa.* . . .

"Maybe you should keep your pants buttoned," Masa retorted. He smiled, showing teeth too big for his mouth, but there was a challenge in his voice and the smile was just a twitch of his lips. "I wouldn't stir that Anaïs's pot for nothing. From what I hear, she ain't exactly a woman. Maybe she's even a *rezu* like Gabriela. Maybe you like that, huh?"

His mouth twitched again. Snowflakes hit the incisors and expired.

I didn't like being with Masa when he had a weapon. After all, Masa was that rare animal on Mictlan: a killer.

Masa had murdered Kiichi Koda-Schmidt back in 96, shooting him in the leg and then bludgeoning the crippled man repeatedly with a convenient hunk of shale until his face was an unrecognizable pulp. Evidently, the two had argued while out hunting, and the argument had turned both physical and and deadly. Old Anaïs, Ana's Geema, had been judge for the trial. No one was much surprised that Masa had killed someone, nor that Kiichi was the one dead—both men had demonstrated evil tempers in the past, and neither had demonstrated any inclination to control them. No one was even appalled by the lame excuse Masa trotted out—the quarrel had begun when he and Kiichi couldn't decide who was going to eat the last bit of sugarpaste in their packs, and Kiichi (Masa claimed) had tried to brain Masa with the same rock first; they'd also both been roaring drunk when the fight started.

People have been killed for poorer reasons, I suppose, and Masa seemed genuinely remorseful afterward, though that was no doubt small comfort to Kiichi or the Koda-Schmidt family.

If the triteness of the reason for Kiichi's murder wasn't enough, what really pissed off old Anaïs was that Masa had left behind the game they'd killed, choosing to lug back Kiichi's body instead.

"It wasn't enough to kill a man," she told him, and her anger honed the voice until it cut. "You had to see if you could *starve* a few of us at the same time. You're not only violent, you're stupid."

Had Kiichi been a woman, Masa might have been summarily executed for the murder—there being no excuse for that level of stupidity. But Kiichi was a male, and thus not overly valuable. Instead, Anaïs had declared Masa shunned for five years.

Shunned. The word itself made me shiver. I can't imagine the isolation one of the Shunned must feel. For five years Masa performed field work. For five years, all his communal and conjugal privileges were revoked. For five years, no one—under penalty of being shunned themselves—would even speak to him or acknowledge his presence except when absolutely necessary. He was given just enough food to survive, and had to live apart from all the Families, in the caves near the river.

For five years, Masa was alone, exiled in the midst of the Families.

Being shunned could drive people crazy. Kees Allen-Levin had been shunned for two years for stealing food. During SixthMonth, he walked to the summit of the rock. There, with only the Miccail stelae to see, he'd thrown himself from the high cliffs. Samuel Koda-Schmidt had vanished into the wilderness before his shunning was over; Lynnèa Martinez-Santos had been shunned for only six months, but afterward, she was never the same and died within a year.

And Gabriela Rusack, the first one ever shunned, and shunned not once but twice . . . well, that's a tale we all know, a cautionary fairy tale told to children from their infancy.

In the year since the restoration of his position, Masa had been in a few altercations, but they'd been emptyhanded affairs, none serious enough to cause the Families to ask old Anaïs to shun him once more. Still, no one—not even his Family—wanted to be around Masa alone. Wangari Koda-Shimmura had started a pool to see when he'd finally step over the line again.

I didn't particularly want to be the reason to change Masa's status quo—definitely not when the man was armed.

"Nei. You're my role model, Masa. Didn't you know that?" I grinned back at Masa, and left him to chew on that— I figured it would take him a while to work it out and see if it came out to an insult.

We were sweeping the fields near Rusack's Trail for grumblers. After the attack on Euzhan and the way the grumbler came at Anaïs and me, a lot of people were understandably paranoid about the creatures, and Kim-Li Allen-Levin had spied a mating pair of them prowling the fields this morning; Johanna, her Family's matriarch, had insisted that the grumblers needed to be chased away or killed, especially since this was a Gather night. No one argued with her, not even Dominic. We've all seen how quickly Mictlan's creatures can change.

The Family Elders tell tales of the redwings filling the sky each autumn; it used to be their sign that it was time to begin the harvest. Now, barely seventy-five years later, redwings are rare. When I was born, there were summer bloomings of piercing white blossoms on the sweetmelon vines along the

59

edges of Tlilipan, and they always swarmed with small, electric-blue curltongues, lapping at the flowers with their long, namesake feature. Now the curltongues ignore the sweetmelons, preferring instead the midges clouding the air above the black water. And we've all seen how the land barnacles changed their patterns from bright purple to stone brown in the course of less than a decade, as soon as they decided to infest the compounds rather than the trees around us.

For that matter, snow had usually been pale yellow until six or seven years ago; now it is more often this iron-oxide red. That's just a few examples. Anyone could give you a dozen others. Nothing on Mictlan stays the same for very long. Nature seemed to have gunned the twin motors of mutation and evolution here. Grumblers suddenly turning aggressive?—it wasn't much of a leap.

So we plowed on between the rows of faux-wheat, dusting ourselves with colored snow.

We spotted grumbler spoor about ten minutes later: brown-black droppings near a crumpled section of wheat. Masa crouched alongside the scat and carefully prodded the nearest mound with a wheat stalk. The stalk went in easily, and as soon as the surface was broken, the *khudda* steamed.

"Fresh," Masa grunted. "The sons of bitches are right here." He straightened, looking at the lines of wheat. We both saw the line of crumpled stalks at the same time, not twenty paces ahead. The grumblers had pushed through the row down which we were walking, heading toward the river. The stalks were rising back up as we watched. "Right fucking here," Masa repeated in a hoarse whisper. He unshouldered his rifle and checked the chamber. The metal bolt snapped back into place with a oiled, sharp *clack-clack*. I checked my own weapon, remembering the way the grumbler had come at Anaïs, remembering the way the beast had torn Euzhan open.

We followed the trail.

The grumblers must have been moving fast, probably scenting us in the field. The knot in my stomach loosened slightly—that was typical grumbler cowardice. With any luck, we'd find that they'd hit open ground and bolted for the cover of the forest.

We weren't graced with that kind of luck. I came out of the wheat field a few steps ahead of Masa. The grumblers had halted out in the strip of open meadow between the field and the river trees. It was snowing harder, and I blinked into the bloody flurries. The grumblers were staring back at me, a female and her pup, with the mam making the standard mumbling challenge as I emerged, though she was still backing away as she growled and chittered in my direction, pulling her youngster with her. Kim-Li had said there were three of them, but it looked like daddy had already taken off.

Masa came huffing out of the field about then. "*Khudda*," he said when he saw the two, and his rifle snapped up. I pushed the barrel up and over before he could squeeze the trigger. "Hey!" Masa shouted. "What the fuck—"

"There's no need to kill them," I said. "They're leaving. Let them go."

"You're joking."

I still had hold of his rifle. "I said, we let them go if they want to go. Fire a few shots in the air if you want to get them moving, but I don't see any need to kill them."

"You still say that after what happened to Euzhan?"

The female grumbler was still backing, still facing us, her dreadlocked chin—longer than the male's—wagging with the motion. She pushed the child in back of her with her hand, and the gesture looked no different than something we might have done, trying to protect the children from some threat. "*Hai*," I told him. "I still say that."

"Then let go of my rifle."

I let go. Masa put the stock on his shoulder, the barrel pointed up at the ruddy clouds over the grumblers' heads. I should have known, but before I could move, Masa brought the rifle down sharply, his finger coiling around the trigger. The female went down in a heap with the explosive report of the shot. Masa laughed. "Damn it, Masa!" I shouted.

Daddy grumbler came hurtling out from behind us, howling. He hit Masa from behind, cloth tearing as the beast's claws dug into his coat, and both of them went down, the grumbler tumbling as it hit the icy ground. Masa's rifle went flying somewhere off into the swirling snow. Masa shook his head, groggy; the grumbler was already on his feet.

I shot him. He went down with a hard thud. The youngling grumbler was howling now, snarling and hissing near the body of its mother.

There was a third shot, and the pup crumpled, silent. I looked at Masa, who'd recovered his rifle. He cocked his head toward me, still sighting down the barrel. " 'They're leaving,' " he said mockingly. " 'Let them go.' I'll be sure to remember that, Elio, next time."

Masa's face, twisted and distorted in fear and distaste as he looked down at the body of the grumbler, reminded me of something...someone...For a long time, I couldn't think of where I'd seen that look before. Then, as he grimaced and turned away from the carnage, his eyes narrowed and hard, I knew.

His was the look Dominic had worn this morning when we talked about Anaïs: the same unfocused anger, the same loathing of the unknown, of the different.

SHADOWS

Elio Allen-Shimmura

"HERE'S WHAT I'VE MANAGED TO RECOVER FROM what's left of the Miccail's stomach," Anaïs said to Máire Koda-Schmidt. The two of them were poring over some greenish sludge in the bottom of a vial. The bog body was lying on a gurney in front of them; to me, it looked like nothing more than a squashed mud sculpture. Máire glanced up as I entered, giving me a sidewise glance that barely registered my existence, her attention all on Ana. Máire's the closest thing to a biologist we have. She works with Ana and her *da* Hui often, and I wasn't surprised to find that Anaïs had asked for her help with the bogman.

Máire's a bit of an oddity herself. Like Anaïs, she's one of the few women in the colony who have never managed to at least become pregnant, if not to actually deliver a child. I've been to bed with her three or four times over the years—pleasant if not particularly enthusiastic sex. She doesn't seem to ask anyone much; that, coupled with the fact that she's often at the clinic with Anaïs, has led to a few whispered rumors. As far as I know, the rumors—like most of their ilk—have no grounding in truth.

Anaïs saw me as well, and even through the mask I could see the muscles of her face tighten, even though she kept looking at Máire. "All this was in the stomach, not the intestines, so it's his last meal, eaten just before he was killed. I've looked at it under the microscope; there are grains of some sort, but I thought you might tell me exactly what."

"I'll give it a look, Ana," Máire said. "Give me a few days for the workup. I'll let you know when I have it."

"I can't say that it looks particularly appetizing," I interjected, mostly so they couldn't ignore me anymore.

"Elio," Máire said, finally acknowledging me. The greeting seemed colder than usual. I wondered if she and Anaïs had been talking. Máire glanced back at Anaïs, held up the vial. "I'll check this out first free time I get," she said, then brushed on past me on her way out, tossing her mask and gown into the hamper.

Anaïs and I stood there for a few seconds trying to pretend that neither one of us was uncomfortable.

"I was in visiting Euzhan. Hui told me I could come in here. 'She's in with her new toy,' he said. Strange toys you have. Me, I always played with blocks."

I think she almost smiled; at least her eyes crinkled slightly above the mask. Her hands were covered with thornvine gunk and some other stuff I was fairly certain I didn't want to identify. "You want to help?"

My face must have given me away. I could see her mouth lift beneath the mask in what I hoped was a smile, and she continued. "No, not with this, Elio. There's a tattoo on the body that I'm fairly sure represents something. I made an ink drawing. I need a research librarian—and you're the person handling the databases. Maybe you can make some sense of it."

I glanced at the ugly sack of dark flesh on the table, glad she wasn't asking me to touch it. "I'll try. There's some stuff of Gabriela's on file that may help. Where's your drawing?"

"In my office. I'll get it after I finish here. I hear you and Masa killed some grumblers this morning."

I grimaced, remembering. "*Hai.* A whole happy family of them."

She looked at me strangely, dark eyes wide over the mask. "Good. We wouldn't want anyone else hurt like Euzhan. She's doing well, by the way. I almost let her go home today, but with the Gather tonight, I thought she'd be better off here rather than worrying your Family with her. She'll need to be watched carefully for the next few weeks, and we have a saline drip in her that someone would have to change. I'm still worried about infections . . ."

She was talking too fast, chattering, not wanting to give either of us a chance to change the subject. She realized it at the same time and stopped. "Hui already told me about Euzhan," I said. "That's not why I came in here."

"Elio, if this is about the other night—"

I interrupted her. "I was an ass."

Her eyebrows arched and then sagged. She didn't argue with the statement. "Elio, I think it would be better if we both pretended it didn't happen."

"Neither one of us can do that, and we shouldn't need to. I wanted to know . . ." I stopped. My fickle, prepared explanation had made an escape, without even leaving a word track behind. ". . . if you were all right," I finished lamely. "I shouldn't have left. I'm sorry."

"I asked you to go, remember?" She shrugged. "You went. No apologies needed. It's over."

Words as percussive as rifle shots. Bang, bang, bang. I grunted with the impacts.

"I just wanted to know—"

"Wanted to know what, Elio? Didn't you see enough? Wasn't that enough for Dominic, wasn't that enough proof that I'm unfit to be with anyone from his Family, man *or* woman? It's done, Elio. You don't need to know or say any more. The rest is going to stay private . . . at least that's what *I'm* intending." She looked down at the bog body and reached for an instrument on the tray next to the gurney. "Right now I have work to do."

"So do I. At the moment, I'm working on my apologies. Obviously, I need a lot of practice. Anaïs, I'm very sorry."

Her hands paused somewhere above the Miccail body. The tip of the scalpel was trembling, shivering as light from the blade sparked on her gown. "You didn't *do* anything, Elio."

"I know. That's the problem."

"Elio, this isn't about you."

"I was there, Anaïs. That makes me involved. You haven't talked to your Family, have you? You haven't talked to anyone. What I'm saying is that if you'd like to talk, I'd like to listen."

"No, Elio," she said, her gaze on the bog body, and then she finally looked back up at me. "There's no need for us to pretend, Elio. I'm not hiding anything from myself, not trying to forget what happened. I appreciate that you asked me to sleep with you again, but it's obvious that I'm . . ."

Despite her claims, I saw Anaïs choke on the next word, her face all screwed up as if she were about to cry. Then she caught herself, and slid a mask over her emotions, drawing herself up with an audible intake of breath. Everything was suddenly locked up and shut away, so that the words just dropped out like empty shells. Even her eyes above the gauze were empty.

". . . deformed. I'm sorry you had to be there when I found out just how bad it is. It's a mistake I won't make again."

"When *what* happened, Ana?" I prodded, rudely. I didn't care. I wanted to see something shatter the barrier she'd so quickly erected. I wanted to see something move inside her. I wanted her to cry or laugh or get angry—*anything* but just stand there and talk like she was discussing last night's dinner. I didn't know why I wanted a reaction, why it was so important to me, but I did. "What was it? You didn't want me to help, remember? What happened, Anaïs?"

Her eyes flickered: *anger?* "Get out," she said. "Now."

"Anaïs, as a friend—"

"Is that what you are, Elio? Or is all this protestation just some nagging guilt? I saw your face the other night, remember? I saw horror and disgust—you can't deny that it wasn't there. I *saw* it." Then the barriers closed in again. She picked up an instrument from the tray and leaned over the bog body. "I understand it, too. Now . . . good-bye, Elio," she said.

"What if you're wrong about how you think I feel, Ana? What then?"

My words surprised me as much as they did Anaïs, I think. I wasn't sure where they came from or what they meant. I didn't give either of us a chance to meditate on them, either.

"I'll see you at the Gather tonight, Ana," I told her. "I'd like you to be there."

I turned and left before she had a chance to answer.

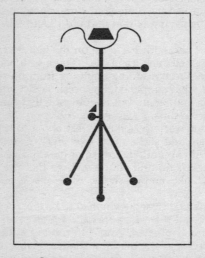

Elio—Here's that sketcho of the tattoo.
Anaïs

CONTEXT:
Maria Allen-Levin

%% "WHO ARE YOU GOING TO BRING BACK TO YOUR
room after the Gather, Maria? Domi, or maybe
Ben?"

Havala had finished brushing Maria's hair. Maria fastened
the buttons of her favorite blouse, then picked up a crystal
of yellow quartz attached to a leather thong and placed it
over her head. She glanced at herself in the mirror, taking
care not to smile too broadly and show the dark gap on the
left side of her mouth, where she'd lost another tooth. She
was on her third set of teeth now, and Hui had told her that
he thought he could see another set following. *"That's why
your mouth is set so low, so there's room for all those teeth. Think
of it as a blessing—you'll never be a toothless old woman.'*

"I don't know, Havala," she said. "I think I'll just see
who's wearing yellow."

"Marshall's older, but he's very . . . interesting."

Maria laughed. "So is *he* the one . . . ?"

Havala rubbed her stomach, which rounded slightly over
the waist of her pants. She leaned over Maria to lay the brush
on the table, and Maria saw her sib's hands. Mottled green-
gray patches of dry, scaly skin ran under the cuffs of her
blouse. "Maybe. Probably. And if he is, you might have the
same luck."

"No wonder Marshall's been so popular lately."

Havala smiled at her sib in the mirror and hugged her
from behind. "I'm so happy for you, Havala," she said. "I
have a feeling about this one—a good feeling."

"So do I," Havala whispered in her sib's ear, and Maria
caught the hint of sadness in her voice. Havala had been
pregnant twice before, miscarrying early both times. Maria
knew how that hurt; she'd miscarried herself, a half year
ago. *The sudden blood, the cramps and pain, the tiny, poor
thing . . .*

She forced the thought away. A Gather was for happy thoughts. A Gather was for optimism and hope. She held onto Havala, clutching her tightly, and then letting her go reluctantly. "Come on," she said. "Let's go see if we can make sure Marshall gets a yellow stone."

VOICE:
Elio Allen-Shimmura

LONGAGO IS THE HERALD OF A GATHER, WHENEVER that nearest of our two moons rises full in the eastern sky at sunset, looking impossibly huge and yellow. This time, Faraway graced us with her ephemeral presence as well, a pale eye peering above the rim of its brighter, closer sister moon. The snowstorm earlier in the day had passed through; I could see sky between the clouds.

By the time the western horizon had performed its slow shift from orange to ultramarine and the first stars emerged between silvered clouds, the six fires were lit on the old landing pad—now swept clear of snowdrifts—and the Families burdened the makeshift tables with food. Tozo Koda-Shimmura started a slow beat on the massive ceremonial drum built by the patriarch Shigetomo Shimmura, a low booming throb that slammed into your chest, forcing you to breathe in time. The drumbeats sounded like the great earthquake tread of some giant walking the earth. Tami Koda-Schmidt, our community *Kiria*, donned her orange robes and—walking slowly as befitted her age and position—anointed each of the fires with spicewood as the drum continued to sound, sending the strong fragrance of rich earth drifting with the smoke.

When she'd finished and the last reverberations of the drum had faded, ancient Vladimir Allen-Levin, as the eldest member of our community, shuffled forward with a caged curltongue, its iridescent blue wings fluttering as the cage (the steel bars crafted from a broken shovel belonging to the original exploratory mission) swung back and forth from

Vlad's wrinkled, arthritic hands. Kiria Tami reached into the metallic prison and tied a long strand of thread around the curltongue's left leg—the thread was made of interwoven human hair, one strand from each of the Families. When Tami finished, she slowly paraded the curltongue around the cracked concrete perimeter of the pad to the accompaniment of the drum's slow cadence. Finally, at the pad's center, Tami lifted the protesting curltongue high as Tozo hammered hard at the drum.

She released the curltongue.

We all watched it dart away into the twilight, losing sight of it quickly as it bore each of us, symbolically anyway, away into the sky with it.

Our rituals are—at most—a hundred years old: a single breath of time for the ancient genes residing in our bodies. To me, the customs don't resonate the way they should, with layered, vibrant timbres from lost ceremonies and prehistoric symbolism, with voiced echoes passing from generation upon generation upon generation. Even the old religious ceremonies brought from Earth seem out of place here. In coming to a new world, we lost our connection to the old ways, our roots. We've had to make new celebrations, new festivals, new rites and passages. We've had to delve for the part of us that is of Mictlan, and that's still a small portion of the whole.

Of course, that's me. My feelings. If you ask Dominic, he'd tell you that everyone is incredibly moved by the ceremonies we've created. He would insist that they are as impressive and evocative as those of the far older religions our ancestors followed.

I don't know. Maybe he's right. I seem to be one of the minority who don't feel a sense of release as the curltongue flies away, who doesn't sense the presence of the *kumi* in the thundering voice of the drum.

I watch the ceremony. I pretend, but I don't feel. It all just leaves me empty, and I wonder why.

Somewhere over the immense slanted rock into which the First Generation had carved the settlement's tunneled home, I lost sight of the curltongue. A collective sigh rose from those around me, but for me it was more relief than release. Off to one side of the pad, Thandi Martinez-Santos began to beat a quick rhythm on her *bodhran*, a compelling, insistent beat that was joined quickly by flute and guitar.

71

Someone began to dance, and then another, and that broke the spell the ritual had cast. People began talking and shouting and laughing, and dancing shadows lurched and prowled out over the night-wrapped fields around the pad. The area seemed incredibly, impossibly crowded with the eighty or ninety people milling around the thirty-meter square of concrete. I felt almost claustrophobic, surrounded by the rest of my kind. The noise level alone was incredible: the music and conversation, the stomping feet and clapping hands of the dancers, the laughter and shouting.

"Quite a show, Historian," someone commented at my shoulder. "You'll have to write it up."

I turned. The speaker was a woman, someone I didn't recognize, which made me gape like an astonished child for a moment. Then a tide of static washed slowly over her auburn hair and down the tea-colored, round face and lush body under a long wrap. "Hey, Ghost," I said, and noticed then that someone had dragged one of the projectors down from the Rock—probably Ché Koda-Levin, our astronomy buff, who monitors Ghost's orbit. He would have known Ghost was due to show up tonight. "Yeah, it's a good turnout."

"Your ancestors back on Earth wouldn't have thought so." Her voice was a sultry, slow alto. I liked it. I wondered who she was, this person in whose shape Ghost had cloaked herself. One of the original ship members, probably, as they were Ghost's usual choices. "They'd have thought this looked pretty sparse. In fact, this would have looked sparse even in the *Ibn Battuta's* central hall."

"My Earth ancestors wouldn't have been able to name every other human on the planet on sight, either," I told her. "I can. For us, this is urban blight."

Ghost grinned and favored me with a seductive tilt of her hips. The first song had ended, but the musicians were already striding into another energetic jig that pulled at least half of the people out into the central circle. Their mingled breaths made a thin white cloud above the pad. In the cold evening air, steam rose from the sweat on their arms.

"Hey, Elio! Hi, Ghost." Ama Martinez-Santos interposed herself between me and the crowd, holding out a large, ceramic bowl. Inside, on the polished aquamarine glaze, loops of leathern strings coiled around colored stones. "Choose," Ama said to me. "Maybe you'll get lucky." Ama was wearing a similar necklace herself—one of the red and black garnets that occasionally wash up on the riverbank was nestled between her breasts on top of her fur-fringed coat. Ama held the bowl over my head; I reached up and pulled out one of the loops: yellow quartz. She shrugged and didn't try too hard to keep her lack of disappointment from showing. "Ahh, too bad. Becca's got yellow, and Maria, too, I think. Maybe one of them will ask you. Enjoy. Hey, Aris!—you need a necklace if you plan on getting laid tonight. . . ." Ama went off in pursuit of Aris, and I slipped on the necklace.

"Hey, don't look so forlorn." I glanced at Ghost. She'd added an identical yellow quartz necklace, and her outfit had gone translucent—she'd have frozen to death dressed that way if she'd actually been here. The body underneath looked exceedingly touchable—whomever Ghost was modeling, she'd been a stunning beauty. She licked her lips in mock lasciviousness. "The Gather's just started."

"And you're just a fantasy image. I've dealt with your kind before—lots of times. I can take you on one-handed."

Ghost just smiled at that. "You know the rules: a man's not allowed to turn down a woman with a matching necklace during the Gather."

"That's *your* custom. I've read the transcripts. You were the one who suggested this little ritual to the Family elders."

"I was just trying for some random mixing of the gene pool," Ghost replied. The necklace was gone, the blouse was opaque and buttoned up to the neck. "It's my job."

I fingered my necklace. "And you think this works."

The grin looked more mischievous than anything else. "Probably not. But it does add some spice to the evening, doesn't it?" Ghost seemed to sense that I was searching the crowd, looking at all the faces caught in poses of flirtation and enjoyment. "I don't see her, either," he said.

"Who?"

"I downloaded and read all the personal files as soon as I relinked," Ghost said. "Like you, the person we're talking about generally writes everything down."

"Ahh."

"If it helps, I'm talking to her right now at the clinic. Is there anything you'd like me to relay?"

So Anaïs was at the clinic, which meant that she wasn't coming to the Gather. Nothing changed. The bonfires didn't dim, the music didn't suddenly go muffled. But I found myself frowning. "No," I said. "I don't think so. I'm going to wander, Ghost. Listen, I've about caught up with the hardcopy on the last download from the ship. You might want to dump another transfer into my terminal."

"I'll do that now. Enjoy the Gather."

I didn't answer. I wandered off into the more crowded areas of the pad around the food tables. Someone handed me a mug filled with dark, thick beer from the tap. I nibbled on the pastries arrayed on the tables and watched the dancers, nodding in time with the music.

"Why aren't you out there?" Máire had come up alongside me, holding a beer herself. "It's one way to stay warm on a night like this." Over her coat, an amethyst swayed below the leather necklace. Again, I didn't notice any particular disappointment that her stone didn't match mine.

"Not in the mood, I guess."

Her eyebrows arched slightly at that, and she took a sip of her beer. The song ended, and appreciative applause drifted up toward the twin moons and the stars, following the trail of sparks from the bonfires. People moved around us, laughing and talking as they headed toward the tables. "Not in the mood, huh?" Máire said. "Or hasn't the right person asked yet? Maybe the right person just isn't here?"

Dominic came up to us before I could answer, leaning heavily on his cane, and peering up at the two of us through disapproving, dark eyes. "Elio, Máire," Dominic said. "I trust everyone is enjoying themselves." His words came out encased in a breath of fog, and I could see his gaze moving from my necklace to Máire's. He almost smiled then, belatedly.

"I'm having a great time, Geeda. In fact, I was just about to ask Máire to dance with me. So if you'll excuse us . . ."

I put my mug down on the table and held out my hand to Máire, who looked at me suspiciously for a moment. Then, her lips pressed together, she set her mug alongside mine and took my hand. We headed out toward the dance circle as the musicians broke into a gavotte. We moved silently through the intricate steps of the dance for several moments, weaving through the other couples in the circle. I'm a two-left-footed dancer, especially with something that complicated, but Máire compensated wonderfully, making me appear almost graceful. Dominic, who glared at us for a long time, finally turned his back and started talking to old Vlad and Kiria Tami near one of the bonfires.

"Why do I feel like I was just used to make a point?" Máire whispered as the steps of the minuetlike dance brought us close for a moment.

"A sudden impulse," I told her. We moved apart, then together again. Her hands were colder than the beer mug. Her attitude seemed only slightly warmer. "I didn't mean to drag you into a Family spat. Thanks for going along with me."

"The truth is that I don't like your Geeda very much." We moved apart, took two lilting steps hand in hand to the left, then came together again. "Sorry," she added, but there didn't seem to be much apology in the voice. "I don't mean to insult your Family."

"Dominic doesn't make liking him very easy." The gavotte took us across the circle as we took new partners for a few measures, then returned. "It's a talent he has. He works at it very hard."

"You can tell him that his practice shows." That came packaged with a fleeting smile, and I grinned in return.

"He'd just take it as a compliment."

That brought another smile, one that lingered a little longer than the last. We didn't say anything for a time, saving our breath for the dance. After the swirling, energetic flourish of the final movements (where I had to be rescued at least twice), we applauded the musicians and headed for the side again as new dancers entered the circle. "I know who you were waiting for, Elio. I'm sorry I'm not Anaïs," Máire said as we recovered our mugs. "I was hoping she'd come to the Gather, too. I really didn't think she would, though. Not after—" Máire stopped. She sipped her beer, looking out at the darkness over Tlilipan. She shrugged.

"Not after *what*? After what happened with me? I'd be curious what Ana told you."

"She told me enough to know that she doesn't want it discussed." The glance she gave me then was strange, a flashing of dark eyes in the firelight. I wasn't quite certain how to decipher the expression. "For what it's worth, Elio, she cares about your Family. Especially Euzhan. She cares about you, as well—about what you think, about your feelings."

"She has an odd way of showing it."

"I know she thought about being at the Gather. Actually, I thought she'd come, but . . ." Another brief shrug. "She's a very private person. For good reasons." Máire blinked as a stream of smoke from one of the fires drifted between us.

"I know her reasons."

"Do you." Máire said it flatly, so that I couldn't tell whether it was a question or not.

"*Hai*," I answered. "I do." I frowned, looking out at the dancers, at the flirtations, at the people who had already coalesced into couples for the evening. I should have been happy, seeing that. I wasn't. I fingered the yellow stone around my neck, lifting it slightly. "Máire, ummm . . ."

"No," she said. We both knew what I'd been about to ask. "I don't think so. Not tonight, anyway."

I nodded, trying to pretend—as our customs dictated— that it didn't matter. "Yeah, we don't match anyway."

"No," Máire answered. "We don't match."

There didn't seem to be much to say after that. Máire, after a small noncommittal smile, drifted away toward the food table. I wandered some more. Becca had seen the yellow stone on Hizo's necklace and paired up with him; Maria was with Marshall. It was a good night for yellow, it seemed— not that it mattered for me. Danda had yellow also, but very obviously didn't take any notice the times I walked past her. I don't know what happened to Máire; she disappeared not long after our dance. So had Ghost, the *Ibn Battuta*'s erratic orbit once more taking her out of range of our patchwork equipment.

In another hour, the fires had gone to burning embers and most of the couples had drifted back up to the Rock and their beds. A few of the elders were still there, huddled around one of the fires and talking with themselves. Dominic was among them. He looked up once from his conversation, and saw me. Disgust pinched the corners of his mouth as he glanced at me. Elio: The Failure. The Ugly.

I walked slowly away from the remnants of the Gather, heading back up the path to the Rock.

I went to bed alone.

INTERLUDE:
KaiSa

"YOU'RE THE LAST, THANK VEISATI," THE YOUNG
Sa said as KaiSa and AbriSa stepped into the
boat. The child had introduced kerself as BelSa—ke was no
one that Kai recognized, evidently an acolyte who'd come to
the island in the last three cycles while Kai had been away.
Bel was a handsome child, just balanced on the edge of ad-
olescence. Bel's strong muscles moved under ker *shangaa* as
ke paddled the boat away from the rocky shore. *If Bel com-
pletes the rites*, Kai thought, *ke will do well Outside. A handsome
Sa indeed*.

The sun flickered through fast-moving clouds, the play of
light and shadow across Kai's *brais* causing ker to shiver un-
comfortably. KaiSa looked back at the shore, draped in mist
in the cold morning. Somewhere back there was a danger.
Ke could sense it, growing each day as ke and AbriSa had
made their way back toward the AnglSaiye. Kai didn't know
what the danger was, but ke could feel it, pressing down on
ker soul.

Soon they would know the shape of this nameless fear.
KaiSa looked out to the bay, shielding ker eyes against the
salt spray kicking up over the long, intricate curves of the
carved bowspirit that protected their craft from the demons
of the water. AnglSaiye, home to all Sa, loomed ahead of
them: a craggy presence, a jagged crown of darkness sitting
between the light grays of the sea and sky and stretching
most of the way across the bay's narrow mouth. The wind,
cold and cruel, lifted the long swells of the endless ocean
and hammered them against the rocks there, giving the island a skirt of white foam. Faintly, Kai could hear the sea
bells sending their greetings, the iron clappers on the great
bronze bells moved by the waves as they crashed into the
island. The familiar sound woke memories of when ke'd last
been here, the tidal bells sending ker farewell as ke left
AnglSaiye for the world ruled by Te and Ta.

"All the other Sa have returned, then?" Kai asked Bel. The youth nodded silently, saving ker breath for the effort of leaning into the oars as a wave lifted the bow of the small craft.

Bel's face was grim, drawing lines that should never be in the face of one so young. "All," ke breathed, "except those that JaqSaTu believes will never be coming back."

With that, Abri shivered alongside Kai, a cold that was more than that of wind and sea. *What has happened out in the world?* Kai wondered. *Who can't return, and why?* "We'll know everything soon enough," Abri said, guessing at Kai's thoughts. "Listen to the sea bells. There's such power in their sound. . . ."

Someone saw them as they approached the island. Guiding fires were lit on either side of the island's harbor, their orange glare illuminating the lower banks of the mist. Call drums boomed out a challenge from the high cliffs of AnglSaiye; Kai went to the small call drum mounted below the bowsprit and responded, giving the coded rhythms that identified the three of them in the boat, letting those on the island know that they were in no danger.

NasiSaTu, the legendary Sa who had by kerself defied the customs of that time and created the Community of All Sa, had led them to AnglSaiye. Only once in its long history had AnglSaiye been attacked—by the army of the mad KeldTe. A thousand boats, each carrying two hands of warriors, had covered the waters of the bay, intending to invade the island, which had become home to the Sa only five hands of cycles before. The foundations of the White Temple had just been laid; its great concourses and gardens were still under construction.

KeldTe was determined to break AnglSaiye and bring the Sa back under the control of the Te and Ta—or, more truthfully, of himself.

That had been the darkest moment in the history of the Sa. The Sa were not warriors, and the TeTa would not or could not work together in concert to smash KeldTe. The Sa had nothing but the protection AnglSaiye itself offered, and their prayers.

VeiSaTi was a god who required sacrifice. NasiSaTu had prepared kerself. As the Sa called upon the god VeiSaTi, NasiSaTu had stood on the cliffs of AnglSaiye, with all the Sa beseeching ker not to do this. Ke only smiled at them, and then let kerself fall into the water, into the hands of VeiSaTi.

VeiSaTi had been pleased with the gift of life. A great storm arose the next morning, scattering Keld's boats and breaking them into tinder on the rocks. Those few of Keld's army who reached the island safely died there on the pebbled beaches, slain by the long spearblades of the Sa before they could even begin the long climb to AnglSaiye's heights. Keld himself was never found, drowned in the storm. NasiSaTu's successor, saddened by the useless carnage, had left the island the next cycle to bring peace to a sundered land, giving back to Ta and Te the lands that Keld had stolen, building the High Road that linked them all, and sending out the first mendicant Sa—the travelers.

Six *terduva* ago, that had been. 3,072 cycles of relative peace had come and gone; nearly thirty hands of SaTu had ruled the island after NasiSaTu. Seeing AnglSaiye brought back all that long history to KaiSa. Ke watched the island grow larger, and glimpsed the White Temple high above through the mists.

A few moments later, the drums answered with permission to land. BelSa leaned heavily into the oars once more, moving their boat through the swells and into the calmer waters of AnglSaiye's harbor.

A trio of Sa was there to meet them as they bumped the wooden dock. BelSa tossed a rope up on the dock; the boat was quickly secured and hands reached down to help them up. Kai and Abri each knelt and picked up one of the rocks, spat on it, and tossed it into the water—the ritual of all Sa who return to the island, giving of themselves to the water, which was VeiSaTi's domain. The three Sa who had met them had just completed their First Vows and the rituals that formed their new commitment to VeiSaTi: all wore beaded gauze masks over their faces, hung on copper frames so that only their eyes could be seen, indicating they had entered their cycle of silence. Their bare chests were newly marked with the sign of AnglSaiye, their skin inflamed and red around the blue-black markings that represented VeiSaTi as well as the world of the Sa. Kai knew two of the three, and ke nodded to them in recognition; ke recalled ker own cycle of silence, and how difficult it had been, yet at the same time strangely pleasant. One of them pointed toward the long stairs cut into the living rock of AnglSaiye, twisting upward and disappearing into the mist.

"Yes, we're ready," Kai told them. "BelSa, many thanks for bringing us home."

Bel inclined ker head as ke finished securing the boat to the dock. Kai took a breath and grinned briefly at Abri. The stone stairs sagged in the middle, worn away by countless Sa feet. Kai remembered the first time ke'd seen the stair, as a child. Ke'd been awed and frightened, and as they climbed, ke found kerself hugging the cliff, frightened by the dark heights that seemed to go up forever. "Home again," ke said. "I'd forgotten just how tall the stairs were."

"So had I," Abri answered, "but we'll remember quickly. Our thighs will remind us."

There were five hundred and twelve steps from the beach and up the cliffs of AnglSaiye to the emerald and satin slopes above. They were not given any rest as they climbed. Kai's legs and lungs burned with exertion long before they caught their first glimpse of the roofs of the White Temple, set near the cliff's edge and overlooking the bay.

When they'd reached the summit at last, all of them paused to take a sip from the deep well, fed by the temple spring. The water was frigid, with a sharp metallic aftertaste that instantly brought memories back to Kai. Wiping ker lips as ke slowly regained ker breath, Kai glanced up the short slope.

There, the White Temple gleamed, snared in drifting sunshine.

The White Temple had been formed of AnglSaiye's pale marble, the massive triangular blocks quarried from deposits on the sea-face of the island and then laboriously brought here on rollers. The curved face of the temple was a reminder of the feminine part of the Sa, while the central spire mirrored the male essence. Standing on the temple stairs and looking down toward them was a familiar figure.

"JaqSaTu," Kai cried, and immediately gave a sign of obeisance, covering ker *brais* with one hand.

JaqTe returned the gesture, more perfunctorily as befitted ker station. Ke strode down the stairs toward them while acolytes scattered out of ker way like startled *kasadi* along the edge of a spring pond. "KaiSa, AbriSa," ke said as ke approached. "It's good to see the two of you. Praise VeiSaTi. I was afraid. . . ."

JaqSaTu had changed much in the cycles since Kai had last seen ker. Ker hair had taken on the silvered hues of age, and deep folds had settled in along the lines of ker face. Ker teeth were marbled with dark lines, and the eyes had a tired look, as if ke were not sleeping well.

"JaqSa, what is going on?" Kai asked, unable to restrain ker curiosity any longer. "Calling the traveling Sa back to AnglSaiye—that's never been done before. I thought . . ."

Jaq held up ker hand, but the stern gesture was belied by the slow smile that shaped ker mouth. "KaiSa, I can see by your eyes that you're thinking the cycles haven't been particularly kind to me, but *you* haven't changed at all. You still lack patience." Jaq's smile disappeared as ke looked past Kai, Abri, and their escort, and Kai turned to gaze with Jaq out over the green-gray waves of the bay toward the land. "This much I can tell you now. What is out there is the ghost of KeldTe. He has returned once again. Not the man himself, but the sickness that was in him. That spirit has found yet another host."

CONTEXT:
Máire Koda-Schmidt

MÁIRE COULD STILL SEE THE FIRES OF THE GATHER flickering through the trees down on the landing pad. The moonlight was bright enough that she could see figures moving on the path between the Rock's main gate and the pad. Her room was in one of the towers springing from the Rock, and the open window brought the smell of wood smoke and the faint sound of people talking. There were other sounds in the night as well: the chirps, burbles, and peeps of Mictlan's wildlife, and once the distant, deep growl of a grumbler. Below, from her sib Kim's room, came the grunting, high-pitched panting of intercourse. Máire wondered who Kim was with; she seemed to be enjoying herself, with whoever it was.

Her sib's cries of passion stirred an echo within Máire's own loins. Still standing at the window, she reached down and lifted the hem of her nightshirt. She slid soft fingertips through the curled forest between her legs. The first touch brought a surprised, gasping inhalation. She closed her eyes, sighing and giving herself over to the urgent, rising need within her. A fragrant wetness responded to her touch, and she let her mind roam, let it seek the fantasy it wanted.

She knew who it would be. She knew. She told herself she didn't care.

When the orgasm rolled through her a few minutes later, she let herself collapse against the windowsill. With the waves that shivered through her body, she whispered the name softly to the wind, to the night, to the world.

There was no answer for her, and when the last shudders had passed, somehow she felt emptier than she had before.

INTERLUDE:
KaiSa

LATER, AFTER THEY'D RESTED, THEY CARVED THEIR names on one of the numerous *nasituda* of Returning Travelers set before the Temple, and urinated carefully on their glyphs. New *shangaa* of unbleached flaxen were given to them. The ritual purifications took the remainder of the night: first the uncomfortable purging, then the pleasant, warm salt baths and the perfumed oils. Kai spent time cleansing the interior of ker pouch, which still smelled of the infants ke'd held there while the Ta and Te, Xe and Xa had gone about their tasks. The scent brought back painful memories of mingled joy and despair, the blinding thrill of seeing ker children born of Ta and Xa, and the utter misery and anger of the leavetakings. The odor seemed to linger for a long time on ker fingertips.

Around ker, in the community rooms behind the Temple, eager and clumsy acolytes attended to other needs of the Sa, as Kai had once done kerself. There must have been three hands of hands of traveling Sa gathered here—more of them than Kai had ever seen together in one place. Yet there were faces that Kai missed. "Where's Loiti?" ke asked of ker peers.

"Ke went out four cycles before I did. Or Karm? I don't see ker . . ." There were no answers to those questions, only shrugs and grim silence.

Ke talked softly with the others, some of whom ke knew, many more ke did not because they had been traveling since before Kai had come to AnglSaiye kerself. They traded tales of their experiences, all tinged with the sadness that Sa shared as their birthright. They avoided the topic of why they had returned to the island, though Kai knew that it was uppermost on all their minds.

By the time the meditations were finished and they were cleansed enough to enter the Temple, Kai had sipped ker cup of bitter *jitu* and gratefully sank into the receptive half-trance the brew granted. Ke walked with the other Sa to the White Temple, through the milky glow of Chali and into the searing ocean-roar that was the massed choir of acolytes behind the mucca-shell partition at the rear. Their voices shivered in Kai's mind, colors cascading from the falling tones.

When the LongChant had ended, JaqSaTu moved to the gigantic, unbroken whorled shell that the founder NasiSaTu had found (impossibly) where the White Temple now stood—VeiSaTi, whose birthplace was in the depths of the sea, had placed it there as a sign to NasiSa. The smooth mouth of the shell stole the smoky yellow light of the torches and transformed it into rainbowed splendor. A distorted, elongated image of Jaq was reflected back at the ranks of Sa in the pearled, natural mirror.

"Sa!" JaqSaTu cried, and the word echoed in the vast Temple's interior. Kai shivered as if suddenly cold; alongside ker, Abri noticed ker discomfort and took Kai's hand comfortingly. "VeiSaTi Kerself has called you here, not me. Ke has spoken in my dreams, in my meditations, and Ke has said that we must prepare to defend the way of life Ke has given to all Sa."

With that, Jaq unfolded the tale that had brought them all back to the island. "His name is DekTe," Jaq began. "Some of you may have given children to his father and mother, CeriTe and LaiTa, in cycles past."

"I knew CeriTe and LaiTa," one of the elder Sa said, one of the travelers unknown to Kai. "Ceri was stern and unhappy, and walked with a terrible limp from a fight with a neighboring Te, and Lai was a mirror to him, reflecting his own bile back to him. I did what Sa do, and left before the children were born. I was happy to be gone from there."

"DekTe is definitely his father's child, then," Jaq responded. "And he has taken a Ta who matches LaiTa: her name is CaraTa, and we are told that she is as fey as DekTe. We also know that at least one Sa who has ventured into their territory has not come back out again."

Jaq raised ker hand against the massed uproar those words caused. "Please," ke said. "Listen to me. We know that DekTe and CaraTa have taken up the mantle of KeldTe. A cycle ago, emissaries came here to AnglSaiye. They told us that Dek and Cara had armed their Xe and Xa, and attacked along their northern and eastern borders, taking lands that did not belong to them. We know that TeTa have conflicts, but this was no honorable *xeshai*. They killed the TeTa who ruled there without letting them offer ransom, and broke their *nasituda*. The XaXe who fought against him were captured, and Dek freed any of the JaJe who would swear loyalty to him."

It might have been the heat in the White Temple, or the *jitu*, but as JaqSaTu spoke, the air around ker seemed to waver in Kai's vision, and in the reflective surface of the god's shell, an indistinct figure started to form. Kai cried out in surprise, and Abri clenched ker hand tighter. "Do you see it? Do you see it, Abri?" Kai asked ker, whispering, but Abri only shook her head.

JaqSa didn't notice the apparition forming around ker, either. Ke continued to speak, ker tone weary, as if the very words exhausted ker. "We know that KarmSa was in one of the territories they attacked. Dek and Cara ignored our laws, and despite the fact that Karm was Sa, they would not let ker leave. Dek gathered together all the XaXe he had captured, and he and Cara. . . ." Emotion overcame JaqSa. Ker head bowed, and it was a long moment before ke looked up again. "This is difficult to say. They mutilated KarmSa in front of all the XaXe. They said that they would do the same to any Sa who opposed them."

The figure around JaqSa coalesced, darkened. To Kai's eyes, it seemed to be a Sa, but impossibly tall. The smoky, indistinct hands lifted, ker *brais* was a blue fire, and ker eyes were white.

They stared directly at Kai, and the triple gaze burned.

But only Kai seemed to notice. Only Kai saw ker. JaqSaTu continued to speak, oblivious.

"KarmSa took ker own life afterward. DekTe and CaraTa have recently attacked and won another territory, still moving northward—toward AnglSaiye. They are now near Black Lake."

Another howl of fury. JaqSa raised ker hands in supplication as the apparition behind ker did the same. Kai trembled. "That's deliberate provocation on the part of Dek and Cara. They know that Black Lake is sacred to us, and they look to draw us out from AnglSaiye. They also have thousands fighting with them now, more than KeldTe ever had. The XaXe who have come to us, fleeing from them, say that Dek and Cara have said that any Sa belong to them. Sa children have been born but not sent here to AnglSaiye for evaluation and training."

Kai hardly heard the words. The apparition continued to stare at ker, and now the hand lifted and one long finger jabbed imperiously at Kai.

Against the rising sound of Sa outrage, JaqSaTu lifted ker own hand. "I hear your anger. I feel it also, but the laws we follow are clear on this, and I don't pretend to be as wise as NasiSaTu. So I'll follow ker path. From this point, no Sa will serve DekTe and CaraTa, or anyone who follows them. If they persist in their actions, we'll call for all Te and Ta to join us against them, as NasiSaTu did with KeldTe. This time, we hope, they will help us. What remains is for someone to take this proclamation to DekTe and CaraTa. After what they did to KarmSa, I can't ask any of you to do that. I can't, and I won't. I will go myself, and you will elect a new Tu after I am gone."

There was a quick roar of protest. In the clamor, the apparition jabbed ker finger once more toward Kai. Kai released Abri's hand and stood. As ke did so, the apparition dissolved, melting into a cloud that rushed to Kai on some unfelt wind. The cloud struck ker in a numbing cold, the cold of the deep sea. Kai shivered as ke raised ker hand to speak.

"I will go, JaqSaTu," Kai said. Ker words sounded as if someone else were speaking them, far too powerful for ker own voice. "You're needed here. VeiSaTi has called me, and I will go."

JOURNAL ENTRY:
Gabriela Rusack

I THOUGHT THE WORST THAT COULD POSSIBLY HAPpen to me occurred when the *Ibn Battuta* exploded, tearing me apart from Elzbieta forever. Elz and I had been partners for so long, friends for even longer, and I loved her so intensely that it wasn't possible for me to think about life with her. We were *one*. We were twinned souls.

But when the *Ibn Battuta* was destroyed, I was here on Mictlan, and she was up there on the ship. I thought that nothing, *nothing* could hurt me worse than that. I don't even know how I managed to get through those first few weeks, and for months afterward, a word, or a smell, a taste, a song . . . all sorts of odd things would trigger memories of Elzbieta and I'd start crying, feeling her loss all over again. I believed it would always be that way.

As it turned out, I was wrong. I never stopped loving Elzbieta or missing her, but time eventually grew scar tissue over the wound, and I found that a new wound always hurts worse than an old one.

Worse was the ostracism that came later. Worse was being ignored by nearly all the other people around me. Worse was never again knowing the soft touch of someone else's hand or mouth.

And worst of all were the taunts of the children, who I knew were only mirroring what their parents—my old shipmates, whom I'd once counted as friends—taught them. *Rezu*, they called me, making the word sound like a curse. *Old Crow!* they shouted. They threw stones at me when they saw me; they made up cruel rhymes.

> *Gabriela rezu, nasty old crow*
> *Gabriela rezu, dying in the snow*
> *Let her lie there until she's blue*
> *Gabriela rezu, we don't see you.*

The only reason I bothered to stay alive was the pleasure I derived from being a constant reminder to them of how cruel they've become.

VOICE:
Elio Allen-Shimmura

I COULD HEAR ANA AND MÁIRE'S VOICES BEFORE I actually entered the Allen-Shimmura common room, all underlaid with the atrocious caterwauling of Gabriela Rusack's music. From what I could tell, they were discussing the bog body. I stopped outside the door for a moment.

"... a coarse porridge of grains, a *meuslix*. As best as I can tell, anyway."

"So he made a bowl of cereal, and then they hit him over the head, strangled him, and threw him in the lake just to make sure he was good and dead. Maybe he was the cook."

Máire chuckled. "I'll admit it wasn't much of a last meal. What surprised me is how crudely ground it was; from the husks, dirt, and pollen mixed in, I'd guess that it was hastily plucked and then quickly prepared, especially since you tell me that Gabriela found some old Miccailian millsites which were quite sophisticated. Your bogman's cereal wasn't very tasty—by our standards, anyway. But ..."

"But?"

"Well, if that supposition's right, if his last meal was harvested just before he was killed, then from the pollens and grains that were present we can place the time of the year he died: autumn, probably late—just about this time of year. There were puffwort spores mixed in, and they're just blooming in the last week. Of course, that's assuming puffworts bloomed at the same time back then. Here ... try this. Now don't make faces like that, Ana—it's your scientific duty...."

I could hear the clink of a spoon against pottery. Then Ana sputtered. "Gods, Máire, that's ... that's *awful*," she said. "I'll bet he *was* the cook." They both laughed.

The sound released me from stasis. "So what's so awful?" I asked, and entered the room.

"Elio . . ." Anaïs set down a bowl of assorted stems and grasses floating in thin, blue-white goathen milk. She pointed at it and made a face. Máire didn't look as if she were pleased at my intrusion, or maybe she was just mirroring Ana's expression. "That concoction is what Máire is telling me my bogman ate just before he died. Want to try some?"

I grimaced. "If he ate that, then I think you need to add another cause of death."

"It wouldn't kill you, Elio," Máire said, but the look she gave me indicated that she might not mind if it made me ill. All the sparkle and humor had drained from her voice. "In fact, you could live fairly well, if boringly, on a diet of this."

"Not to mention that you'd get your yearly quota of roughage and fiber in just one sitting. No thanks. I leave the experimentation to the scientists. You're the experts."

That seemed to finish the conversation. For several long seconds, we all looked at each other with polite half-smiles while we tried to think of a neutral subject. I was about to ask about Euzhan when Máire sighed and rose from her seat. "I need to get back," she said. Her hand was on Anaïs's arm; Anaïs put her hand on top of it.

"Thanks for your help," she said to Máire. Anaïs smiled at her, then Máire nodded and gathered up the various grasses and mosses that she'd brought.

"I'll talk with you tomorrow," she said. "If you want."

"I'd like that."

Máire smiled at Ana, just looking at her for a few seconds. Finally, almost with a start, she turned to leave. We both listened until her footsteps faded down the corridor. Just as they did, Anaïs's *mi* Keri started to walk into the room, saw the two of us alone, muttered something neither one of us caught, and left. "Popular place," I said.

Anaïs shrugged. "I'm sorry, Elio. I wish they wouldn't do that."

"It's okay. My Family would have done the same if we were there."

"Would they." There was no rising tone at the end of the sentence. Instead, it was weighted with a ponderous nonchalance. She'd picked up the bowl of the bogman's cereal and was holding it in her lap, one hand on the spoon.

"I was sorry you weren't at the Gather the other night. I'd hoped you'd come."

She watched me, not saying anything, Gabriela's music a monochromatic backdrop. She lifted the spoon, dropped it back. The metal rang against the lip of the bowl. "I was busy."

"I'd like to know who you were avoiding: me, or Geeda Dominic and his entourage?"

Her eyes cut a swath over my face. Her fingers went white around the spoon. I didn't say anything. She started to speak, looking up again at me, then biting her lower lip and looking down again. She punched the spoon into the cereal. "You can't understand," she said. She was holding the spoon in her fist, like a dagger. She stabbed at the mess in the bowl. "You just can't."

"Probably not. But I'm listening."

"Is that supposed to make me feel better? Since you're willing to listen, is Dominic going to change? Maybe I can just stand outside the complex and shout 'Praise all *kami*, Elio's willing to *listen* to me!'—that'll certainly have an impact."

The spoon jabbed at the cereal again. She blinked hard, looking away from me. A tear traced a wet line down her cheek, and she swiped at it with her free hand, sniffing. "All I want . . . Damn . . . *Damn*. . . ." She stopped. More tears stole from under her closed lids; this time she didn't do anything to hide them. "I didn't ask to be this way. I didn't have any choice in how Mictlan twisted me."

I could hear the spoon grinding against the fibers in the bowl. Anaïs stared at the bowl, but I knew she didn't see it. "I never meant for Ochiba to be anything but happy. She *was* happy. We both were." A stab of the spoon. Another. "And for that . . . for that . . . most of the people here would treat me like . . . like the fucking Miccail on my slab."

She threw the bowl on the floor. It hit the stone flags and shattered, spewing chips of glazed pottery and milk-soaked grain. The Family's verrechat, which had crept into the room, went streaking away in panic. Anaïs was sobbing, great racking breaths, her hands cupping her face. I sat on the couch alongside her. I touched her shoulder. When she didn't pull away, I slowly gathered her into my arms. She tensed for a moment, then her body relaxed and she leaned into me, still crying.

We sat that way for a long time.

VOICE:
Máire Koda-Schmidt

~~ I LEFT ANAÏS, AS ALWAYS, FEELING VERY CONFUSED.
You'd think I'd be used to it by now, but I'm not.
I doubt that I will ever be.

Part of me—the part molded by Family and society—was
hoping that Elio and Anaïs would go to bed again, that it
would finally work between them, and that Anaïs would be
happy. Part of me was just . . . well, the only word is jealous.
I was also angry with myself for leaving when I wanted to
be the one to stay.

And part of me was simply frightened of the conflicting
emotions.

Damn, damn, *damn*. . . . So confused. . . .

This is certainly not what I expected. The person I see
looking back at me from the mirror isn't ugly (nor, honestly,
is she beautiful). I'm not visibly deformed like Elio, Anaïs,
or most of the others. If I'm not particularly drawn to any
of the men, well, I don't find any of the *other* women attractive either.

Attracted to Anaïs? Loving Anaïs? That makes no sense.
It makes no sense at all.

Hell, I *want* children, as much as any other woman here.
I want to experience the sensation of life growing inside me;
I want to push a new life out between my legs and hear her
first cry. I want to hold my babies, to hug them, love them
and watch them grow. I want to become Geema myself, to
have my children's children running and laughing around
me. I want some part of me to go on, forever.

And I want Anaïs, also, in a way that scares me.

I'm betrayed by my own emotions, and there isn't anyone
to talk to.

Off to the west side of the old landing pad there is a cemetery. I go there sometimes, when I want to converse with
myself. All of the Matriarchs and Patriarchs are buried there,
along with their sons and daughters, and most of the sons

and daughters of the next generation as well. I no doubt share blood with most of them, at least in some little part. I go there and touch the headstones, and try to feel the connection. I try to talk to their *kami*, who surely must lurk there.

There are other headstones, too, and they far outnumber the others. These are small stones, the majority without names: the graves of our children, the ones dead before they tasted the fullness of life. I wander there too, at times, and I look at the names carved there, and the dates:

FEMALE CHILD OF NICOLE KODA-LEVIN
BORN ON 37 FEBRUARY 27
DIED 37 FEBRUARY 29
WE LOVED YOU. REST WELL, DEAR

Two days old, this infant, and she was plucked from Mictlan by disease or some unrepairable genetic defect, without even a name. Or . . .

PIET MARTINEZ-SANTOS
B.85 AUGUST 40
D.90 JANUARY 12

. . . who at least made it past his fourth birthday, despite the terseness of his epitaph. I even remember Piet. I remember how he died of pneumonia, gasping, coughing, his lungs slowly filling with mucus until he drowned in his own fluids, while Hui and his mam, along with his *mi* and *da*, watched helplessly. I don't need an inscription to know how they felt.

I look at the graves and I remind myself that Mictlan is a cruel, awful world. I tell myself that I'm *lucky* that I haven't brought any children into it. *How can the mothers stand it?* I wonder. *How can you invest so much love and care and hope into a child, only to see it die as an infant. How is it possible for a mother to survive that? Doesn't the death of your child leave you broken yourself? How can you look at your child and know that the odds are that she'll never reach adulthood, that this world will most likely reach out and snatch her away from you, screaming in pain, fevered and sick? How can you croon to your baby as she suckles your breast, in full realization that we won't even give her a name until she's passed her first birthday, just because so few of them make it that far?*

How could you want children, knowing that? How can you look at the quiet rows of white stone and not refuse to be part of the cycle? How can you still say "I want to give life"?

But you do. I do. I leave the cemetery with tears for the lost ones' *kami*, but with that need still festering inside.

I touch their graves, these lost cousins of mine, and I cry for them, and I tell myself—like all the other women—that *my* children would live. That *my* love would keep them alive.

I even know I'm indulging in the worst self-delusion, and I don't care.

CONTEXT:
Tami Koda-Schmidt

TAMI SAW MÁIRE WALKING PAST HER ROOM. AN IM-pulse made her call the girl in, gesturing. Máire, a lab apron wrapped around her, came in, tilting her head questioningly, her hands plucking like nervous birds at the waist of her apron. She wrinkled her nose at the smell of incense burning in the altar before which Tami sat.

"I'm sorry, dear," Tami said. She blinked, trying hopelessly to clear away the eternal haze of the cataracts. Her voice trembled, as did her entire body: a persistent, constant motion. That was her birthgift from Mictlan, to have muscles that were never at rest, never totally under her control. She put her hands in her lap, clenching them tightly in a futile effort to stop their shaking. "I just haven't had a chance to talk with you since the Gather. I wanted to know how you thought it went."

As she spoke, Tami watched the face of her great-granddaughter carefully. There was the faintest flicker of . . . *disdain? or just discomfort?* . . . before Máire smiled. "You were the best Kiria I've ever seen, *Mi* Tami. I thought the ceremony was especially beautiful."

Tami had to smile in return. Máire was—truth be admit-ted—one of her favorites, and Máire's smile had neutralized many a childish wrong within the household over the years. There had always been something wild and rebellious about the girl, but her intellect was keen. Máire been a challenge, in nearly every way, to her teachers within the Family. It had been Tami who advised that Ghost be allowed to set the curriculum for Máire, and that she be apprenticed to no one. That had created an angry and painful confrontation with Gerard and Eleanor, the Geeda and Geema of the Family. *Everyone* was apprenticed—that was how crucial knowledge and crafts were passed down from generation to generation. "You'll be wasting the wild girl, Tami. Half the Families already think we've ruined her. No. She'll be apprenticed and that's the end of it . . ." It had taken all of Tami's coercive skills to convince Gerard and Eleanor that Máire had new talents to offer.

And the "wild girl" had proved Tami right. It was Máire who realized that the stringy webbing choking and killing the faux-wheat crop was produced by a suddenly mutated version of the formerly innocuous insect they'd named the leaf-biter, and that introducing pincer beetles to the fields would control the leaf-biter population. After that, Máire had been left to roam wherever her interests took her, and no one within the Families much questioned her contribution to their society.

Yet. . . .

Tami worried about Máire, worried about her seeming lack of interest in the settlement's all-important reproductive task. She wondered why Máire, unlike the rest of the young women of her age, had never really indulged in the sexual freedom their society encouraged. Tami wondered, even if she refused to let those speculations actually form into words in her mind. If those vague inner nudges became thoughts, she would have to act on them. "You wore your amethyst to the Gather, didn't you? I noticed Chi-Wa had picked an amethyst from the bowl," Tami said.

"Yes, he did, *Mi* Tami. I saw him with Thandi later on."

"I saw you dancing with Elio."

Emotions flickered behind Máire's eyes. Tami could see them, but Máire gave them no words. Behind the smile, her voice was empty. "Yes, we did, *Mi* Tami. He's not much of a dancer, though."

Tami knew that Máire had come back unaccompanied from the Gather, of course. There were no such secrets in a Family compound. *Just a matter of bad karma*, Tami told herself. *The* kami *weren't with Máire.* She would pray to them later; she'd give them incense and spices. "Overall, he's a good child, Elio. Studious. Paper everywhere in his office. But good. I think he would be a decent lover for someone."

"Yes, *Mi* Tami," Máire said, but there was no agreement in her voice. "*Mi*, I need to check on an analysis running in the lab. . . ."

"Yes, of course, child. I won't keep you. It was only. . . ." Tami stopped. She closed her eyes for a moment, letting the smell of the incense calm her. "Máire, both you and Elio see so much of Anaïs. I'm . . . I'm worried about her. So are others, Dominic, for instance. Anaïs won't come to see me on her own, but I *know* something is troubling her. I'd like you to tell me what it is."

Máire's face was arranged in that careful neutrality. "*Mi*, Anaïs's problem is that she works too hard. If she's not taking care of someone, she's trying to learn more about that Miccail corpse Elena found."

"She's also not coming to the Baths, and from what I've heard, she's always careful to stay fully clothed, even around her own Family."

Máire was shaking her head. "*Mi*, who here *doesn't* have some defect? Half the colony can't metabolize one kind of food or another, and most of us have some physical mark." Tami saw Máire glance pointedly at Tami's hands, still clenched in her lap.

"Máire . . . dear. . . . Yes, minor genetic variations are entirely common—skin blemishes and unimportant quirks. But we're not talking about those."

"Aren't we?"

"That's what I'd like to know."

"*Mi* . . ." Máire loosed a sigh of exasperation. "I have to wonder *why* you're asking me this. What if I told you that I knew that, under her clothes, Anaïs is like some awful monster? What would you do about it? What possible difference would it make? Are you really worried because you think something is 'troubling' Ana, or are Dominic and some of the other elders suggesting something else? That's who started you on this, isn't it?"

"Máire, dear . . ."

"I'm sorry, *Mi*. I know you have responsibilities as Kiria. I know the Elders have their concerns, also. But there's nothing right about hatred, especially based on ignorance. Not here. It's bad enough that we gave in to that once before with Gabriela. There's so few of us, Mi. I don't care what Ana is, what she believes, who she may love or how she loves them." A blush darkened Máire's face. Tami could almost feel the heat of it. "*Mi* Tami, I have that analysis. I need to go now. I'm. . . . I'm sorry."

Máire ran from the room, the apology in her wake. Tami sat there for long minutes in the haze of incense, wondering what it was that Máire was apologizing for and hating herself for wondering.

VOICE:

Máire Koda-Schmidt

I WENT TO THE CLINIC A FEW DAYS LATER. Anaïs had scraped some dirt samples from the bog body's skin that she wanted me to examine, and I thought I'd pick them up. My *da* Hui was there, checking on Euzhan and making sure that Hayat was still awake. "Máire," he said. "Anaïs isn't here."

I can never tell what Hui is thinking. I know that Hui is one of the few people Anaïs would call a friend, and I know he realizes what Ochiba was to Anaïs. He's also has made it very obvious to everyone else that he doesn't care. Yet . . . I think his protest is part denial. I think he's more bothered by it than he will say.

" 'Evening, *Da*. I know. She's with Elio, I think."

I suspect he knows how I feel about Anaïs, and there's that one important difference: Ochiba wasn't Family. I am. I know that changes things for him, even if he's never said it—funny how much more tolerant we are of the behavior of others than those who are closest to us. I can't tell whether he's angry with me, or just somehow disappointed, and he's certainly never said. "Good," he said now, flatly, leaving me wondering about the subtext.

"*Hai*. I thought so too."

Another nod, served with a penetrating stare. "How's Euzhan doing, *Da*?" I asked, mostly to deflect the gaze. It worked; he glanced down the corridor to the clinic rooms.

"She's doing well. Anaïs did excellent work, better than I could have done. She'll have a nasty scar to remind her what happened, but I think we'll send her back to her Family tomorrow. Another week or two, and she'll be running around like nothing had happened. You want to see her?"

I went in and said hello. Euzhan is truly a beautiful child. I hated seeing her injured, hated the way she winced when she saw me and tried to sit up. "Máire!"

"Hey, Euz! How are they treating you?"

"Okay, I guess, but I wish Hui and Ana wouldn't frown so much when they look at me."

"I don't know about Ana, but *da* Hui's a natural grump," I told her. "He frowns at flowers." She laughed at that. I hugged Euz, and chattered with her about nothing and everything while Hui—proving my point—gave Hayat a scathing critique of the way he'd changed her dressing. After a few minutes, I excused myself. "*Da*, do you know where Anaïs left the bogman samples she wanted me to check?"

"They're back in the coldroom. You want me to go get them?"

I shook my head and patted Euzhan's cheek. "No. You stay here with this pretty one. I'll get them."

The lights were out. I remember noticing a smell just as my hand reached for the wall plate, something that wasn't antiseptic, sterile, and steel but was instead earthy and animal. I slapped the contact anyway.

It must have heard me coming, because it was already moving as I stepped in. I caught a glimpse of the room, noticing that the cabinet that held the bog body had been slid out of the wall rack, that the sheet that covered it was half off, askew. To my right, I heard a sharp *clack-clack*, like a verrechat's claws skittering on hardwood . . .

. . . and then the side of the room slammed hard across the side of the head.

I must have passed out momentarily. I was sprawled on the floor looking up. A male grumbler was standing over me, one arm still extended—that's what had hit me. I couldn't see out of my right eye, and I could taste blood in my mouth. I was afraid to move—not because of the grumbler but because I was afraid that I might find out that I couldn't. "*Da* . . ." I started to shout, but it came out more a gurgling whimper.

I spat blood. The grumbler took a step back at that, its eyes narrowing and the dreadlocks on the chin waggling. It was ugly, and it reeked. It breathed musk and exhaled decay while it mumbled angrily at me, the claws clashing as it clenched its hands restlessly. I remembered what those claws had done to Euzhan. At the same moment, I realized that I'd fallen between the grumbler and the door, that the grumbler obviously wanted out, and that—prone or not—it considered me a threat.

"You could have asked," I told it, trying to sound as calm and soothing as I could. "I'd have let you out. Really I would have."

It mumbled again, claws slashing air between us. I decided I'd better try moving. I tried to push myself up; that caused the room to do a quick dance around me. The grumbler barked, a percussive sound that hurt my ears. I could hear its claws scratching at the flooring.

"Máire?" *Da* Hui's voice called from out in the corridor. "What's going on?"

The grumbler howled loudly at that. It squinted, the prominent eye ridges folding. It barked at me again, like it was ordering me out of its way. I tried to comply, crawling. Evidently I wasn't fast enough for it.

At least it backhanded me again instead of using its claws. I saw the blow coming this time and brought my hands up to protect my head—it didn't help much. As I went down, as the grumbler leaped over me through a thickening mist, I heard a rifle fire.

CONTEXT:
Elio Allen-Shimmura

ELIO'S "OFFICE" WAS A SMALL ROOM CARVED FROM the Rock by the lasers on the *Ibn Battuta*'s shuttlecraft. To visitors expressing surprise at the sheer amount of paper overwhelming his office, he had a stock answer: "There's an old French proverb I once came across: *Les heureux ne font pas d'histoire*—Happy folks don't make history. There's a hell of a lot of history here."

Most of the time they laughed.

The room had once stored equipment, but a long ventilation shaft had been punched through the stone when this part of the complex had been created. Sunlight poured down the vault to spotlight the desk on which Elio's terminal sat, besieged by cascading piles of paper and books.

"Ana, a lot of Gabriela's stuff isn't in the system—not surprising, given the way most of the Elders felt about her. Still, there were a few things." Elio punched a key and the monitor flickered. "Here," he said to Anaïs, moving one of the piles from a chair and balancing it precariously on the edge of the desk. "Let me clear a place for you to sit. . . ."

Several sheets of paper were still draped over the arm of the chair. Anaïs picked them up, glancing at the title typed there. " 'Transcript of Elders' Monthly Meeting, 101 February 31.' Pretty exciting material you're working with, Elio."

"As dry as dust, and less sustaining."

Ana gave a small half smile. She moved the transcript to the floor and sat.

Kiria Tami, seeing Elio's office once, had remarked dryly that "I know we have a flourishing papermaking industry here. Now I see that you're its sole consumer." Elio could only shrug and laugh. The original colonists would have howled in amusement to see him typing on a keyboard and staring at a monitor, but then they'd had direct neural links to the net and software agents like Ghost. Elio doubted that the Patriarchs and Matriarchs had even *known* how to type. But for their descendants there'd been neither the manufacturing capabilities for the neural webbing, nor the equipment and knowledge to perform the delicate nanosurgery to install them. Elio operated under Ghost's instructions: the computers the colony used were well over a century old, and there were no facilities or expertise to fix anything but the simplest problems. In the last decade, they'd lost a dozen terminals—the dead ones were cannibalized for parts, but at some point in the fairly near future, they would lose their computing capabilities. At that point, they'd also lose Ghost and all the databases on the *Ibn Battuta* as well. Because of that, Ghost and Elio were trying to print out everything they could, so they would have a legacy on the dark night the last computer died.

"I had the system search for the symbols in the bog body's tattoo. Gabriela had tentatively assigned meanings to some of the Miccail pictographs. A wavy line, for instance, shows up on all the Miccail stelae that she identified as birth records. Maybe the curved lines has something to do with a birth, or a beginning. On the other hand, it looks an awful lot like a stylized person: a stick figure. Unfortunately, there's nothing in Gabriela's stuff that talks about a triangle, or about a figure with a tail—if that's what it is. I'm stumped at the moment."

Anaïs sighed. The chair protested as she leaned back against it. "That's it, then. There's nowhere else to check."

"No, not at all," Elio told her. "I have more of Gabriela's journals—not in the system, but handwritten."

Anaïs straightened again. 'I thought all the journals she wrote after she was shunned were destroyed after they found her body."

"Some. Not all. Kahnoch, who was doing my job then, squirreled some of them away. He may have hated Gabriela, but he was fascinated by her, also. And Ghost has some material of hers also, stuff he was able to upload before they purged the system. I'll go through the journals, but that's going to be tedious. Next time Ghost is around, I'll get him started, too. I'll let you know what I find out."

"Thanks, Elio. I appreciate it."

An uncomfortable silence settled around them, broken by the hum of the terminal fan. "I should get back to the clinic . . ." Anaïs pushed herself from the chair, but Elio moved in front of her.

"You don't have to go."

"I do. Hui . . ."

"You've been avoiding me for two days, Ana. If you don't want my friendship, that's fine. But if it's because you don't think I'd want to be with you, you're wrong."

"Elio . . ."

He ignored the hands she raised in protest. He took her head between his hands, drawing her closer. His kiss was soft but insistent. Anaïs, her hands on his chest, pushed against him, relaxed, and then pushed away once more. "I don't know what I am," she said to him. "Elio, Ochiba and I—"

His arm, slicing air, cut off her confession. "I don't care, Ana," Elio told her. "It may matter to others, but not to me. Why won't you believe that? Why won't you give me another chance?"

For a moment, she only stared at him. Then, silently, she took a step toward him. Her face tilted up to his, her arms went around him. Her mouth opened as he leaned into her.

She pulled him down onto the paper-littered floor.

VOICE:
Máire Koda-Schmidt

"... SIT UP SLOWLY. HOW ARE YOU FEELING?"

My *da*'s face came into slow focus, his eyes gray-white with cataracts. I was sitting on the floor, leaning against a wall. Something cold was around my head. I could hear Hayat talking to someone, and Euzhan chattering excitedly down the hall. I shut my eyes and opened them again slowly.

"I feel ... like I fell off the Rock and landed on my head." I moved, and lights flashed behind my eyelids. I moaned, feeling tears start with the pain. I blinked them away. "Do I look like I feel?"

"Pretty much. You'll look worse tomorrow when the bruises show up, and I doubt you're going to be able to see out of your right eye for a day or two. But you're damn lucky. I don't think the grumbler broke anything. If it had used its claws ..."

Neither one of us needed to finish that statement, though it brought back memories. "Where—" I started to ask. I started to get up, but Hui put his hands on my shoulders and pushed me down; it didn't take much effort.

"There," he said, and pointed.

The grumbler was on its back, its long, thin limbs flung out. There was a gaping hole in its chest; blood dappled the floor and puddled underneath it.

"It's dead," Hui grunted.

"Good." I said the word with a savage pleasure that surprised me with its ferocity.

"Was it in *here*?" Da asked, frowning and looking around. I realized that he'd ignored everything else until he'd made sure that I was all right. "Why in the world would—"

He stopped. I knew he'd seen Anaïs's bogman, lying exposed on its slab, its sheet pulled off. He looked from the Miccail to the body of the grumbler.

"Why?" he asked again. "I wonder why?"

100

CONTEXT:
Vladimir Allen-Levin

~~~~ *... THE WIND ... HE HAD NEVER HEARD THE WIND howl so loudly. It seemed like the very Rock itself would shake loose, that the storm would pick it up in hands of lightnings and sinews of thunderclouds and throw them. He could hear something breaking loose somewhere above them, and then a blinding flash and a thunderclap that nearly deafened him. He huddled in a corner of the room, clinging tightly to his mam. Not far off, someone screamed ...*

"Here's your dinner, Geeda."

Vladimir roused himself at the sound, stirring in the worn leather of his favorite chair. Who was it who had spoken? He couldn't be certain. There was someone standing in front of him with a tray, one of the children.... What was her name? Havala? Was that right? Uncertain, he waved vaguely at the table alongside the chair. The girl placed the tray down. "*Arigato,*" he said, and patted her cheek. He couldn't see her clearly, but he thought she smiled as she left. Maybe not. His eyes weren't very good anymore. Most people were only a blur, and even when he recognized them, he often couldn't remember their names.

Vladimir leaned over and lifted the cover from the plate on the tray. Steam wafted up from the meat and vegetables arranged there, but he couldn't smell anything. Food was mostly tasteless anymore. Back when he was a child, when mam Kaitlin cooked, the fragrance alone would satisfy hunger. That was what it seemed like, anyway. He'd come into the common room, and there would be Kaitlin, and her brother Thomas, and grandmam Rebecca, who could speak with Ghost inside her head and who would, sometimes, tell Vladimir and the other children stories of old Earth, stories which seemed like fairy tales, filled with impossibly crowded cities and fantastic technologies, of bloody wars filled with mythical heroes and villains, of despair and hope and sorrow and joy. He loved the stories, even though he wasn't sure he believed them. Once, he remembered, several of the Matriarchs and Patriarchs were at his house for dinner. After Kaitlin had put the children to bed, he'd snuck back into the common room where they all sat around the central fire, drinking and talking, and he'd listened to their voices, feeling a strange comfort in the sound of the adults. He listened to them, without caring that he didn't understand.

"... the truth is that we're already dead. Even if Earth contacted us tomorrow and sent out a rescue expedition the next day, it would be our children's children who are rescued." That was Gabriela, recognizable by her gravelly, husky voice, even in the half darkness. No one sat near her. She was—already—alone. There was a rumble of disagreement around the room.

"All the more reason to put together our breeding program."

"By the blood of Buddha, Robert, you make it sound so fucking cold and sterile. 'Breeding program'—like you're running a damn kennel. Or is it just that you want your own personal harem to screw?"

"Gabriela, we don't need the sarcasm or the crudity." That was Geema Rebecca, her voice colder than Vladimir had ever heard it.

"That's where you're wrong, Becky. We need it because if things don't change, breeding program or not, we're just too small a group to survive. If I have to be crude to make you all listen to me, then so be it."

Another voice intruded. " 'If things don't change . . . ' That's the point, Gabriela. We can't predict change. I say we do what we can, and we trust in fate to do the rest."

"That's nicely said, Jean, and predictably optimistic on your part, but . . ." Gabriela stopped, and turned in her seat. Vladimir hid his eyes and ducked beneath a table, but he could feel her gaze on him. "One of your grandchildren wants to enter the discussion, Becky. He's a little young to be one of the studs in the 'breeding program,' though."

"Damn it, Gabriela . . ." Geema Rebecca's curse nearly gave off heat. She turned quickly to him, and the fury was still in her eyes. Vladimir trembled and shot out of the room, heading for the stairs and his own bed. Behind him, Gabriela's coarse laughter followed . . .

"Geeda, you haven't eaten yet."

Havala—or was it Maria?—was standing in front of his chair, hands on hips. "How do we know when things change?" he asked her. "How do we know?"

The child didn't answer. Perhaps, he thought, there was no answer.

INTERLUDE:
KaiSa

THE BLACK LAKE. . . .
In the legends written down on the oldest *na-situda*, it was said that when the god VeiSaTi emerged from the womb of the WaterMother, Ke stepped out on the land, and where the water fell from Ker giant body and into Ker footprints, great lakes formed. Where three drops—one each from ker male and female parts, and another from ker head—fell together and merged, the Black Lake was made. Thus, the Black Lake contained the triple essence of VeiSaTi, and was nearly as sacred as the ocean itself . . .

. . . for as proof of the lake's holiness, it was at the Black Lake, many *terduva* later, that the first Sa was born, to an unallied couple who had lived on the shores of the Black Lake for several years. Most Sa still were born in the lands nearest the Black Lake, Kai among them.

Since then, the Black Lake was not permitted to be part of any TeTa's holdings. The Black Lake and the land surrounding it were free, open to any CieTiLa who wished to gaze upon it. The Black Lake was a refuge, a wellspring, a paradise. From its shores, no JaJe could be taken forcibly; there, a CieTiLa could meditate on the long path of their history and breath the cool solace of the gods.

KaiSa had been there several times before. Most Sa visited the lake region at some point in their lives—VeiSaTi might be acknowledged as chief among the gods by most CieTiLa, but Ke was crucially important to the Sa, who had inherited Ker form. Walking through the area now, Kai remembered the familiar rolling hills, all blanketed with fragrant net-branches and the crisp brown carpet of their dead leaves. A slow river meandered through the deep, misty valleys—Kai followed its southern bank, where the pilgrimages of generations of CieTiLa had worn a path. Only one thing was different. When Kai had last been here, ke had seen many other CieTiLa. Now, the land was empty, and Kai felt the brooding certainty that the very hills were waiting, and watching.

At the northwest shore of the Black Lake, the river snaked around a huge outcropping of bare stone. Through an opening in the net-branches, Kai could see the *nasituda* set at the summit of the rock. Ke paused, frowning, feeling that ke wanted to crouch, to hide, even though no shadows had passed over ker *brais*. Yet the feeling of uncertain dread remained, prickling ker spine and raising the hair of ker mane.

"I am KaiSa," ke called to the wood, to the rock, to the lake. "I've come from AnglSaiye with a message for DekTe and CaraTa."

There was no answer, unless the wind that swayed the net-branches or the quick rustling of bluewings was a reply. After a moment, Kai took a trembling breath and moved on.

The Black Lake deserved its name. The lake was wide but shallow, and its waters were stained with earth and peat until they were absolutely opaque. The river Kai followed didn't feed the Black Lake, which rested many strides from its banks. No creeks, no brooks, no streams or rills flowed out of the Black Lake, no water flowed in that anyone could see. Still and silent, the Black Lake cloaked itself in dark mystery.

Kai walked along the western shore, ker feet sinking into the marshy ground that surrounded the lake. Dark water filled ker footprints behind ker. Flying insects trilled and darted among the lush vegetation while bluewings floated on the shallows, occasionally darting their long heads down into the water to feed. When ke came to a path, ke followed it up and away from the Black Lake, ascending the southwestern flanks of the granite outcropping. As ke climbed, the feeling of being watched increased, though ke still saw no one.

The sun was low in the sky when Kai reached the flat summit of the massive rock. Ke was alone in sunlight; the land below ker lay clothed in evening shadow. The *nasituda*, nearly twice as tall as Kai, cast long cloaks of darkness over the cliff edge. Ke went up to the nearest standing stone and crouched down to read the lowest carving there:

I, MepTe, declare Black Lake free . . .

"Don't believe what you read, Sa."

Kai forced kerself to stand slowly, ignoring the panic response that made ker want to run blindly away. Ke turned: against the setting sun, a trio of males stood. Kai noticed, most of all, the long killing spears they all held, the pale, keen blades glinting in the last light. Kai spread ker hands wide to show that ke had no weapons kerself. "I am KaiSa," ke said, ker voice calmer than ker heart. "I've come with a message, and I travel under the protection of AnglSaiye."

"I am PirXe," the central figure replied. "And here, Sa, there is no protection unless DekTe or CaraTa wish to give it."

JOURNAL ENTRY:
Gabriela Rusack

I ALWAYS SAID THAT FIREWORKS NEVER HAPPEN. People never really see a stranger across the proverbial crowded room and suddenly have their gazes meet in a splash of instant psychic sparks.

No, I believed that the idea that Out There Somewhere Lives Your Perfect Match was a cruel fallacy. Sparks and fireworks were generally a product of horniness, hormones, and intoxicants, not love. At best, to expect such things was to doom yourself to never finding a relationship that could match your expectations.

That's what I believed.

I attended the first meeting of the potential crew members for the *Ibn Battuta*. There must have been four or five thousand people packed into the Pedro Alvarez Cabral Convention Center in Brazilia. The assorted politicians had made their obligatory speeches, and we were facing an afternoon of excruciating details from the project leaders. The overworked environmental systems were letting far too much of the tropical heat into the building; it must have been nearly 30°C in there. We were all sweating as we filed out into the main hall for the morning break, another discomfort on top of the stress of mingling with a few thousand strangers, since one of the criteria for acceptance was sociability. We were destined to be locked up with each other for years once the voyage began, and you never knew who might be watching you to see how you handled yourself in a crowd. I had just managed to snag a cold drink and disentangle myself from the gridlock around one of the two bars set up in the room, a false smile pasted permanently on my face. I remember pulling my blouse away from my skin, grimacing at the twin circles of dampness under the arms and the wet line down my spine and between my breasts. The ice had already melted in the lukewarm cola.

"Be glad you weren't on the dais under those lights."

The voice held a laugh, speaking English but with the faint undercurrent of an Eastern European accent. I turned, and with the movement, my life changed.

That sounds hopelessly melodramatic, but it was true. I'd vaguely recalled seeing her on the stage with the project leaders. I'd seen the name on her nametag in the program, listed as Infrastructure Team Leader, but I hadn't paid any attention to her. But now.... I knew the instant I saw Elzbieta, saw her strong Polish face and those light, seafoam eyes. Strangely, I understood in that first moment that the attraction cut both ways, and that there was a subtle invitation in the way she held herself. Something inside me gave way, like a key had been turned in a lock, and I *knew*. I swear I did. Elz told me afterward that it was the same for her.

It's strange: I can recall that precise moment so vividly, yet I couldn't tell you what I said then, though I'm sure it was something about the heat. Even when struck with the thunderbolt, we spout inanities through the sparks, and they seem to suffice.

Elzbieta and I went to lunch together that day, with at least a dozen other people, and I couldn't tell you who they were or what we talked about. I only remember Elz, sitting across from me at the long table and occasionally smiling my way. I was dazzled, smitten. Within a week, we were lovers.

So maybe I was wrong. Maybe our perfect mate *is* somewhere out there, waiting for fate to bring us together.

INTERLUDE:
KaiSa

THEY ESCORTED KAI TO AN ENCAMPMENT IN THE forest beyond the southern shore of the Black Lake. By the last light of the day, in a small valley below, Kai saw a sight that terrified ker. There were at least ten thousand CieTiLa gathered there, more than Kai—or any other CieTiLa, for that matter—had ever glimpsed in one place. They sprawled over the valley and up the slopes, a living carpet half lost in the growing night, bristling with spears, the glow and smoke of a thousand cookfires lending a permanent haze.

"There is no hope," Kai breathed. "We had no idea . . ." PirXe laughed alongside ker.

"Still want to speak to DekTe, Sa?" he asked. "Or is this message of yours stuck in your throat?"

Kai shook kerself loose of the spell of ker eyes. "I will still meet with him," ke said. "None of this changes what I have to say."

PirXe laughed again, and pushed KaiSa ahead. In growing darkness, they stumbled down through the trees toward the valley. As they moved through the ranks of CieTiLa, Kai felt their stares, harsh and unfriendly. Kai looked for other Sa as they walked down the hillside into the valley itself. Though male and female were plentiful enough, ke saw none of ker own kind.

After what JaqSa had said, ke had not expected to.

Ahead of them, on a small rise, a large gossamer tent had been erected. The tent was ringed by watchfires, each tended by a guard; another fire burned inside, and smoke curled from a central vent. Through the thin, white fabric, Kai could see figures moving against warm firelight. PirXe answered the challenge of the guards and moved through the fire ring to the front of the tent, one hand on Kai's arm. There, he spoke into the ear of an old male sitting outside the tent's flap. The old one grunted and rose from his seat, going inside. Kai could hear conversation: a male, a female.

Then the tent flap flipped open. Kai blinked. The shimmering light bothered ker *brais*, made ker want to crouch low as a figure stepped out into the night, dark against the flames.

The sight of him made Kai hold ker breath.

"I am DekTe," the darkness said, and his voice was like the low music of the hornshells of AnglSaiye, sonorous and compelling. His was not the voice of a beast, but that of a god. Tall, his arms were corded with ropes of muscle as he folded them over his *shangaa*. Polished stone beads were braided into the twin locks of hair under his chin, and they glistened and clashed as he spoke. DekTe was as impressive as an ancient *nasituda*. And his eyes. . . . Under the ridge of forehead, his eyes and *brais* were the dark blue of late evening, and they reflected the fires as if from hidden, lost depths. "And you are?"

"KaiSa," Kai answered. Ker voice sounded weak against the throb of DekTe's. "I've come from AnglSaiye, sent by JaqSaTu.

DekTe nodded. "It's late. Have you eaten? We have food . . ." He waved a large hand toward the interior of the tent.

"Yes," Kai found kerself saying. "I'm hungry."

"Then come in," Dek said, and there was warmth in his voice, along with what seemed a great weariness. "Come in. You've come a long way, and you must be exhausted . . ."

Kai had thought that ke would meet a monster. This was no monster. Kai had thought that no one could match the charismatic presence of JaqSaTu; ke knew now that ke had been wrong about that, also. Kai felt confused.

Were we wrong? Has JaqSa sent me to the wrong Te?

But no—the army gathered around gave the lie to that. DekTe held aside the tent flap for Kai as if he were one of the Ja. Kai could only nod and enter. Ke hated most the moment when ke passed DekTe, for ke could feel the heat of his body, hear the sound of his breath and smell the musk of his sweat. Kai didn't dare look up, afraid that ke might become lost in those eyes again.

Kai was glad when ke slipped past DekTe into the heat of the tent.

There were two other people in the tent—the old male who had gone in to get DekTe, and a female. She was tall, and there was something in her bearing that made Kai shiver involuntarily. She stepped to one side of the central fire and stared at Kai. "Ke's a pretty one," she said at last, speaking to no one in particular. "But ke looks frightened."

"KaiSa is also tired and hungry, Cara," DekTe said, and Kai realized that this was the Ta. "Ke's come from AnglSaiye with a message from their Te."

"I'm sure we already know this message. But let KaiSa say it and be done."

DekTe smiled—he had a gentle smile, Kai thought, surprised—and gave a soft negative shake of his head. "Let ker eat something first. There's no hurry."

Dek made a short motion with his hand, and the old one, sniffing either from a cold or disdain, went to a small table in one corner of the tent, bringing back a plate of sweetflake and karn-cheese. Kai looked at Dek, who nodded. Kai took a small bite of the cheese. The full extent of ker hunger ripened with the bite, and ke attacked the rest of the food ravenously as the others watched. When Kai had finished the first plateful, more food was brought to ker. Suddenly aware of the appraising eyes on ker, Kai ate the second helping more carefully.

When ke had finished, the old one took the plate from ker. "Thank you," Kai said. They were all watching ker: Dek, Cara, Pir, the old one. Mostly, ke felt Dek's gaze, searing ker face as if with the heat of a fire. Kai took a long breath, calming kerself with one of the mantras from ker student days.

"Speak," CaraTa said abruptly, the harsh syllable shattering the spell of the mantra. "It's late, and I'm tired."

A glance went between Dek and Cara, a silent communication that sharpened the edges of Dek's face, though his features had smoothed once more when he turned back to Kai. "My mate is right," he said. "We're all tired from a long day's march. Give us your message, KaiSa, and I will return you an answer in the morning."

Another breath. Kai closed ker seeing eyes, so that all ke saw was the firelight flickering in the unfocused vision of ker *brais*. "I was given this message," ke said. Ker voice shivered, like a child unsure of a recitation. "What DekTe and CaraTa are doing is against the laws of VeiSaTi and all the gods. You have violated our customs and murdered innocents. In particular, you have ignored the sacred trust that VeiSaTi has given to the Sa. JaqSa, Tu of AnglSaiye and all Sa, would have me tell DekTe and CaraTa that no Sa will serve you from this day forward, nor will we serve anyone who has sworn allegiance to you. Furthermore, if you persist in taking lands that are not yours, AnglSaiye will call for all

109

Te and Ta to join with the Sa against you, as we did with KeldTe long ago. We call for VeiSaTi to protect us, and for Ker hand to move with ours."

Kai waited, half expecting to be struck down. But there was only silence for several breaths.

Then CaraTa gave a quick bark of laughter. "See?" she exclaimed to no one in particular. "Empty threats is all we hear, as we knew. Look at the Sa trembling. Even ke knows it. Well, I know what answer I would give."

Kai saw PirXe move forward with that, grasping for the short knife at his belt. Kai slid easily into a defensive stance, ready to take the weapon if ke could, but DekTe made a motion with his hand that made Pir stop in midstride. "I said we would give an answer in the morning," DekTe said. "We shouldn't be hasty here. Cara?"

Kai watched anger struggling with something else on her face. "Fine," she said. "Ke's hardly important. In the morning."

PirXe, his gaze still on Kai, slid the knife back into its oiled scabbard.

DekTe stepped across the tent until he stood in front of KaiSa. "Does that sound fair to you, KaiSa? Can you wait until morning for our answer?"

He sounded so reasonable, and a wild energy sparked in his words. It was impossible to deny him. Ke might as well deny kerself.

"Yes," Kai answered. "I will wait."

DekTa smiled at that. His hand reached out and almost, almost touched ker cheek.

"Good," he said. He took his hand away.

For the rest of the evening, ker cheek burned.

JOURNAL ENTRY:

Gabriela Rusack

I DIDN'T HEAR JEAN UNTIL HIS BOOT SENT PEBBLES skittering over the edge of the Rock's summit. I looked up from my crouched position; Jean was staring at the Miccail stelae set next to the cliff with something approaching irritation on his face. "Hey, Gabriela ... Ghost ..." he said.

"Well, you don't usually come up here, Jean," I said. "What's the occasion?"

The scowl on his face didn't go away. "How long have we been friends, Gabriela?"

"Depends on what you're asking. If you need some help fetching water or painting, then we've been friends for more decades than I like to count. If you're here about what I think you're here about, I don't even think I know you."

After the first glance back, I hadn't looked at him. I continued to clean the Miccail stele in front of me.

"We've more important things to worry about than a dead race, Gab."

I sighed and dropped the knife I'd been using to clean away the centuries of dirt on the hieroglyphics carved on the stele. "Like what? Like the fact that there are soon going to be *two* dead races on Mictlan?"

He ignored that. "We've been talking—"

"I figured as much. My ears were burning."

"Damn it, Gab, would you give me a chance?"

"A chance for what, Jean? To listen to all the old arguments again and to give you the same old tired answer? Well, here it is, in three little words: I. Don't. Care. I don't care. I lost the only person I loved when the ship blew. Despite the fact that I *like* you, I'm not interested in making love to you or any other male here, in person or with your cold sperm. I never wanted kids. None of what's happened has made me consider changing my mind."

"Gab, be reasonable—" he started, and I cut him off again. Funny how it's always the other person who's being unreasonable.

"No, *you* don't understand, Jean. There are *nine* of us here. Nine. Back on Earth, a species with only nine representatives would be considered as close to extinction as it is possible to get."

"But *not* extinct," Jean insisted. "In desperate trouble, yes, but *not* extinct. Not yet. No one would have given up in that kind of situation."

"Maybe not. But we'd take the remaining members of the species and slap them into zoos and try to breed them in captivity, though—because we'd *know* that there was no way they'd survive out in the wild. Without help, they'd be

111

dead." Ghost hadn't said anything, though I knew he was recording it all. I wheeled around on him. "Ghost, set up this program. We'll ignore the males—it's the females that count. Start with a breeding stock of three women."

"Four," Jean corrected me.

"Three," I repeated, more firmly, and he just shook his head. "Figure that half of any offspring will be male, half will be female—any problem with that, Jean? Fine. Figure two of each three children will reach puberty." I held up a hand to stop Jean's protest. "Actually, I think that's being optimistic. We don't have medical facilities or a trained internist, don't have antibiotics nor do we know if there are plants here that have healing properties for us. Between accident and disease, I think two out of three is being damned kind to us. We're going to see high infant mortality in the first year. My gut feeling is that it's going to be more a fifty/fifty proposition, but let's go with two of three."

Jean just shrugged, so I continued. "All right. We already know that the fertility rate's gone to hell. Figure each female past puberty will produce between zero and five offspring—and before you bitch about that, Jean, remember that we're going to lose mothers and children in childbirth because surgery's going to be high risk, and we're going to have miscarriages that leave some sterile, and we're going to have infertile females, and we don't have the technology to fix any of that. We may have someone who's just the perfect breeding machine, but I doubt it. I think my parameters are pretty close to what we're going to see. You got all that, Ghost? Run random projections based on those figures a few hundred times and see how many generations you get."

"I already have," Ghost said.

"Well?"

I'd have sworn he hesitated. Maybe it was just a glitch in the communications gear. "In all projections I ran, the line died out. The longest sequence was 40 generations; the lowest 2. The average was 7.480 generations."

Jean's mouth was open in soundless protest. "But," he said, and the word hung there for a while between us. "You stacked the figures, *and* you're assuming that nothing changes. Maybe we'll eventually find herbal medicines, maybe with Ghost's help we can set up some of the lost technology. Maybe we'll be more resistant to disease than you think, and the infertility problem—especially if it's due to the LongSleep—may disappear after the first generation or two. Hell, maybe we'll be *found*, Gabriela. Maybe we'll hear from Earth."

"You notice how often you're using the word 'maybe,' Jean?"

"We have to have hope. Things *can* change."

I just shook my head at him. "If you expect humankind to flourish here, Jean, then things had *better* change. They'd better. Otherwise, I don't see that there's any hope at all." I swept my hands to take in the stelae of the Miccail, set here on the Rock ages ago. "There were hundreds of *thousands* of Miccail, Jean, just a few millennia ago. They lived everywhere around here, in a land that they knew and understood, a world that gave life to them, and they're all gone, every last one of them. Two thousand years ago, something happened to them, something that sent them into such a steep decline that when a thousand more years had passed, there weren't *any* Miccail left at all. Not one, out of those hundreds of thousands."

I stooped down and picked up my knife. I started cleaning dirt from the grooves in the stone once more, trying to bring back what time and weather had tried to obliterate. "There are nine of us, Jean. Aliens, all. Intruders. Tell me again about hope."

He didn't answer.

VOICE:

Anaïs Koda-Levin the Younger

AMA, OUR CLINIC "RESIDENT" AND ALSO ONE OF THE midwives for the colony, met me at the door to the Koda-Schmidt compound. She was sweating and her face was lined, as if she'd been in labor herself. Her hands were oily and there was a streak of smeared blood across her forehead. Behind her, I could see the Koda-Schmidt men, gathered in the common room and pretending unsuccessfully that nothing out of the ordinary was happening. I didn't ask

113

Ama the questions I wanted to ask then, but followed her quickly back to Elena's room.

Elena squatted in a birthing chair, supported by Máire and her mother, Morag. Another *mi*, Safia, was massaging her back while Phaedre and Karin rubbed her legs. Elena's black hair was plastered wet against her forehead, and her head whipped back and forth on the pillow. She looked exhausted, panting in the middle of a contraction; everyone else looked just as tired. "Where's Hui?" Morag snapped in irritation on seeing me. "I want Hui here."

I told myself not to get angry. After all, Hui was Elena's *da*. It was understandable that they'd prefer him to me. "He'll be here in a few minutes," I told her. I opened my bag and sat down on the floor in front of the chair so I could see. Máire gave me a quick, apologetic smile; I smiled back at her to let her know that I hadn't taken offense at her mam's comment. "Hui's finishing up—Babacar took a fall in her compound and had to be stitched. How long has Elena actually been pushing?"

No one answered at first. "Since about 4thHour," Ama said finally. She leaned over closer to me, speaking softly. "Anaïs, there's been some meconium, and I don't like the baby's heartbeat. The head's crowned, but she hasn't progressed. That's why we sent for you."

"*Hai.*" I ducked underneath and looked. I could see the head, just crowning: a mass of dark curls spotted with blood and white curds of vernix, and smeared with the oil that Ama had spread over the vaginal lips to ease the head's passage and prevent the vagina from tearing. "Elena, this is Anaïs. You're very close, darling. If you can just open a little more . . ."

Another contraction shook her. Elena sucked in her breath, then shouted. "Damn it, it *hurts!* I can't push it out. I can't . . ."

"Yes, you can, Elena. You can. Think of opening, just like a flower. Relax your face, relax your jaws, concentrate all your energy downward and *open* . . ."

The contraction passed, but the baby hadn't moved at all. Elena's legs quivered, shaking helplessly. I pressed my stethoscope low on her swollen belly, listening. I thought I heard the fetal heartbeat, but it was very, very faint.

I felt more than heard Hui come into the room behind me. His breath was harsh at my ear. "Section?" he whispered.

"Baby's in distress," I agreed. I didn't add '*We might lose them both if we try a section here,*' but Hui knew it as well as I did. "But I think she's close enough if we hurry. Scissors."

Hui handed me the scissors from the bag. I made a quick, short episiotomy. With the next set of contractions, the head finally slipped out into my guiding hands, but the shoulder was jammed hard behind the pubic bone. "Keep pushing," I told Elena. I glanced up at Hui. "Come on," I said to the child, trying to turn it to free the shoulder. I was beginning to feel the first faint crawlings of panic in my hands and along my spine. "Come *on*, baby."

The shoulder popped free suddenly and the child slid out the rest of the way into my hands, as Elena gasped. I didn't like the cyanic color, or the fact that it wasn't moving. *Something very wrong. . . .* The cord was a strange, pale shade and appeared to have collapsed, as if it had been prolapsed.

I saw something else, something that made the room surge around me for a moment as if I were dizzy—the infant was a hermaphodite, the dual genitalia much more pronounced than mine had been at birth. *She's you,* one part of me shouted, while another as quickly clamped down on the thought. *You can't think about that now. . . .*

Hui saw it too. He gave me a strange look I didn't have time to decipher.

She wasn't breathing. I ran a finger around her mouth (somehow I couldn't think of the baby in any other terms than feminine), cleaning it of mucus. I turned her and gave her a solid thump on the back. Still no response. Trying not to curse, I grabbed the stethoscope from around my neck and pressed it down on the tiny chest, hoping to be rewarded with a reassuring, quick *thump-thump-thump*—I heard nothing. I began to sense that crawling feeling of inevitable doom that comes when you know that, in all likelihood, the *kami* are laughing at you. My ears rang with the hammer of my own heart. The world slowed.

It wasn't fair, it wasn't right for her to die. Not so soon.

She was like me. We were kindred. I couldn't let her die.

I started CPR, fingers pushing down on her tiny chest. "Where's my baby?" I heard Elena asking. "What's the matter? Morag, what's going on?"

Morag was shouting too, and Ama was looking confused. I wondered if she'd seen the genitals. "Hui—" I grunted, and I heard him move to intercept Morag as I breathed gently into the baby's mouth and nostrils, talking to them and saying nothing. "Ana's taking care of things. Don't worry . . ."

I hoped he wasn't making promises I couldn't keep. I listened again—still nothing. "Come on," I whispered to her. "Don't do this to us. I'm not letting you do this. Come on . . ."

More compressions, more breaths. She lay there, unresponsive. I wanted Ghost, with his medical database. Morag was wailing despite Hui and Máire's attempts to calm her; Elena was sobbing and moaning, trying to get out of the birthing chair so she could see. "Ama, cut the cord. See if you can get Elena to deliver the placenta. Do it, now." I stopped the compressions, went back to the breaths.

Listened.

Cursed silently.

Started compressions again.

Breathed for her once more.

And this time, this time she gasped, coughed, and wailed. I nearly cried with her. Her limbs flailed, and the bluish tint of her face was replaced by a healthy ruddiness as she squalled. I sagged, the sudden release telling me how tense I'd been. "Is it okay?" Elena was asking. "Ana? Is it okay?"

"She's fine. She's going to be fine."

"She? A girl?"

The question paralyzed me. I should have known it would. Ama was staring. Hui was looking back with his head cocked to one side. I couldn't say anything. I picked up the baby, wrapped it in one of the receiving blankets, and laid her on Elena's chest. Elena, crooning, stroked the matted, birth-misshapen head. "She's beautiful," Elena said, and laughed wearily. She held the baby to her breast; the child's mouth opened instinctively, looking for the nipple. "And hungry, too . . ." Elena guided her, and the baby suckled inexpertly, crying again when the nipple slipped out. "Shhh, darling. Hush. It's okay. It's okay," Elena told her. Morag, Safia, Phaedre, and Karin all huddled around, touching and stroking.

None of them noticed me. Now that it was over, I could be safely ignored again. I knew that wouldn't last long, only until someone decided to clean the baby. Only Máire looked at me, and I knew she could tell something was wrong.

"Ama, would you help Hui finish up here?" I said. Ama nodded. I washed my hands in the basin Ama had brought into the room, and wiped them dry. I stood up, looking at

116

the knot of women around Elena and the baby, trying to decide if I was being too much a coward, retreating so quickly. I just didn't know what to think, what to do. All I knew was that I wanted to be away from here. I wanted to be somewhere alone. I stood and walked to the door.

Only Máire and Hui seemed to notice.

REVELATIONS

CONTEXT:
Tozo Koda-Shimmura the Younger

"Tozo?"

Tozo stirred, slipping uneasily from the space between sleep and waking. Something in Faika's voice sent ice crawling down her spine, and the look on her face intensified the chill. "What is it, Faika? What's the matter?"

Faika only had to utter two words for adrenaline to surge through Tozo's body and sweep aside all weariness: "The baby . . ."

Tozo immediately glanced at the crib set next to her bed; it was empty. She threw the covers aside, slipping out barefooted onto the cold polished stone of the floor as dread gnawed at her soul. "Where is she?" she asked, trying to keep her voice steady.

"Miranda's room. You were sleeping, and she thought she'd take her for a bit . . ." They were running now, padding through the compound, through the common room and up a short flight of stairs to another hallway. Giosha, Morihei and a few others were outside the door of Miranda's room. They stood aside silently as Tozo arrived. Miranda was standing alongside her bed, the baby—Tozo's baby—laying on her back on the quilted coverlet. The tiny chest was heaving, up and down, the labored sound of her breathing laced with phlegm. "Tozo," Miranda breathed, her voice quavering with tears. "She's sounding worse. Should we send for Hui or Anaïs?"

"They can't help," Tozo answered shortly, wondering at the calm in her voice. "Here, let me have her . . ."

Carefully, as Hui had instructed her (as she'd done already too many times in the few short weeks of her child's life) she laid the infant face down over her knees. Gently, but firmly, she struck her back with the heel of her hand, over and over again. *Ghost said that it may be something similar to cystic fibrosis. That sticky webbing she's coughing up is coating her lungs. If it stays there, or if the condition grows worse, even-*

121

tually she won't be able to breathe." He'd looked at her with eyes
that were at once sad and distant. *"I'm sorry, Tozo. I know it's
your first child, and she looked so normal . . ."*

The baby coughed, gagging, and Tozo opened her tiny
mouth, moving her finger around and pulling out a film of
white lace. The lumpy material pulsed on her fingertip, as if
it were, somehow, alive. It was ugly, and Tozo hated it,
hated it because it was ugly and because it was killing her
child. Faika silently handed her a cloth; she wiped the gunk
away and resumed her meticulous pounding.

She remembered her mi *Svati—Faika's mam—weeping uncon-
trollably after Khurseed died in 94 of the Bloody Cough. Svati's
other child, Kuniko, had been born the same year as Tozo, and had
also died of the Bloody Cough at age five. Gayle's son Ghulam had
died at three, after being sick most of those years. He'd never
learned to walk or talk, and though Gayle had cried, Tozo knew
that part of her was also relieved. Her own mam Hannah had four
miscarriages, two before Tozo was born, two after. She'd also
birthed three other children, none of whom had lived long enough
to be named, all dying with a few months. Since the last one, she
hadn't been able to get pregnant at all, though she still tried.
Geema Tozo, who Tozo herself had been named after, had also been
troubled by numerous miscarriages and early deaths, but had
brought five Named children into Mictlan, only to see three of them
die in childhood.*

*Geema Tozo still recited their names in the prayers every Last
Day: Nira, Tonya, and Phillippa.*

Death walked beside the Mictlan's children, and no one
was surprised when they died, but that never lessened the
pain of their loss to their mams. Tozo had thought, as a child,
that she would never understand that kind of hurt, but now
she knew. She knew.

The baby coughed again, spitting up more of the lace, and
her breathing suddenly sounded less labored. Miranda
sighed; Faika laughed in relief, and the family gathered outside the door vanished, going back to their own rooms. The
room shimmered through a sudden haze of tears, and
Faika's arm went around Tozo's shoulder. The baby was crying, too. Tozo opened her blouse and put her baby to her
breast. Tozo comforted her with soft words through the
tears, as her milk began to flow, as the baby suckled.

"It's all right. It'll all be all right, honey. Don't worry. Your
mam won't let you die. She won't. I know I'm not supposed

to do it, but I already have a name picked out for your birthday Naming. I've known it since before you were born. You're going to be Zoe. That means Life. Did you know that? You'll be Zoe . . ."

Anaïs Koda-Levin the Younger

"... EXAMINATION OF THE WOUND TO THE HEAD indicates that the damage was definitely a violent injury inflicted on a living body. The edges are sharply defined, and the margins of the wound are swollen, as they would be if the Miccail were still alive when injured. The clean edges indicate that the weapon was probably something like an axe. I've noticed that the crowns of her . . . umm, his . . . molars are sheared off—probably broken when her teeth slammed together under the impact. The location on the rear cranial protrusion would indicate that the blow was struck from behind and above—maybe she was kneeling when the blow was struck? She might have even known it was coming. The strangulation and subsequent drowning in the lake would indicate some kind of ritualized death— well, it would if we were dealing with humans, anyway. Still, this probably wasn't a death blow, though unless the Miccail were built of sturdier stuff than us, it almost certainly rendered her unconscious.

"The garrote used to strangle him—her—is some kind of animal sinew, knotted three times equally around the loop; I wonder if there's any significance to that? I'll have Máire check the cord to see if she can identify the animal it was made from; maybe that'll give us another clue to this ancient murder mystery. Anyway, the cord's deeply imbedded in the skin, indicating that it was tightened rapidly, closing off the windpipe and eventually snapping the spinal column. The air passages are completely closed. I'd say that strangulation is the probable cause of death, after which the body was thrown in the lake. I'd also believe that—"

I stopped, hearing footsteps I'd known would be coming. I was surprised it had taken this long.

"Mic off," I said, then: "*Komban wa*, Máire." I couldn't bear to turn to confront her, but forced myself to, arranging a smile on my face. I also didn't want to ask the question I knew I had to ask. "How's Elena?"

"Why didn't you say anything, Ana? The way you shot out of there, just handing her the baby without a word . . ." Máire was pacing. Her face was flushed, her brown hair still matted with sweat from Elena's long labor, and her arms swung wide as if she didn't know what to do with them. She stopped, and the anger drained from her suddenly. "Why, Ana?" she asked again, almost crying now. "Why did this have to happen to her?"

"I don't know." It was the only answer I could give her, and I could barely get even those stark, empty words out. Máire's was the accusation I couldn't face back at the Koda-Schmidt compound, the silent condemnation I'd felt when I'd seen the baby. Mictlan had given me a mocking mirror and made me look at myself. "Máire. I . . . The baby nearly died, Máire. Would you rather I'd let that happen?"

Her nose crinkled; her eyes narrowed and flared. "That's not fair, Ana."

"What's not fair is that it's a rare child who's born without some kind of defect. It's not fair that I'm no better equipped than some late-nineteenth-century doctor, that something like what happened today is even a problem." I stopped, holding up hands stained dark with sap. "Máire, I didn't cause the baby to be that way. All I did was deliver her."

"I know that. I do. It's just . . ." Máire looked down at the floor, at the bog body. At me. "Ana, we both know there have been some nasty lies circulating through the Families about you. Don't you see that by leaving you've just made them worse?"

"Not all of the rumors are lies," I answered. "Máire, I can't win this battle. It's not possible. If someone wants to blame me for the baby's deformity, fine—I'll have to be Anaïs, whose very touch causes horrors. Let them say it; I can't stop them. If the baby had died, then I would have *still* been Anaïs the Monster, who kills babies. You think I don't know that, Máire? You think I can't feel the way they look at me or hear the whispers behind my back?"

Máire took a step toward me. I could feel the soft warmth of her hands as they cupped my face. I wondered if she could see the tears I'd scrubbed away before starting to work on the bog body. I wondered what she saw in my eyes.

I wondered what I was seeing in hers. She was so close, and I suddenly wanted more than anything to lean in toward her, to touch her lips with mine . . .

"Ana!" Elio shouted from the coldroom door, staggering to a gawky, awkward halt as he saw the two of us. "Ana, I—"

Máire dropped her hands. My cheeks felt suddenly cold. She was still looking at me, and it was difficult to tear my gaze away to look at Elio. I wasn't sure if I was relieved at his entrance or not. "Come on in, Elio."

"I heard about Elena's baby. I thought maybe . . ." He stopped. Gave us a half-smile that evaporated an instant later. "I guess Máire had the same thought."

"*Hai,*" Máire answered, and it was only after that word that she looked away from me. "I guess I did." She nodded as if to some internal dialog. "El, I'm glad you came. Otherwise Ana would just bury herself in the mysteries of her leathery friend here." Máire inclined her head toward the bog body. "Make her talk to you."

As Máire walked toward the door, Elio called to her. "Máire, you're her friend, too. She can talk to both of us."

Máire looked at me. I think if I'd spoken then, she would have stayed. But I was still wondering at the emotional tangle inside me, still sorting out what I was feeling.

She looked at me and I stayed silent.

"No," Máire said. "I need to get back and see how Elena and the baby are. Ana, I'll see you soon, okay?"

"Okay," I answered. Then, almost too late: "Máire, thank you. Thank you for understanding."

She nodded at that, and left.

JOURNAL ENTRY:
Gabriela Rusack

I WAS MARRIED ONCE, JUST AFTER COLLEGE. I MENtion that so that someone looking at this journal long after I'm dead will understand that my prejudice comes more from experience than hearsay. I fully admit my bias. I know that there must somewhere be exceptions, and I may well have experienced only the exceptions and not the rule. But . . .

I thought Jon was gorgeous: muscular and athletic, with wonderfully sharp cheekbones and strange bright eyes. He was caring, he listened, and he shared. And—when he was angry—he was also physically violent. He hit me. He battered me, the object of his anger. He threatened, several times, to kill me if I ever left him or if I ever told anyone about how he treated me.

I lived with him in a state of constant fear.

After I was finally rid of him, friends told me how Jon had been an aberration, that I shouldn't judge anyone else by the standards he set. I believed them. After I finally left Jon, I lived with other men. My friends were right—none of them ever struck me. But . . .

While watching their furies, I always wondered if they *might*. All it would take was a second, a moment's mistake or loss of control. . . .

In my experience, men are like volcanoes. Some of them are beautiful peaks, quiescent and majestic, but underneath . . . underneath, no matter how well-buried, no matter how benign in appearance, there is a lurking, raging magma.

You never know when a volcano will explode. You only know that sometime, inevitably, it will.

VOICE:
Anaïs Koda-Levin the Younger

I SUPPOSE THAT, ONCE UPON A TIME, I ENJOYED getting dirty. Like most kids, I probably reveled in the occasional mud bath. However, long years of study with Hui in the clinic had turned me somewhat paranoid— I've seen the bacteria lurking in our mud, and I know all too well the ravages of viruses who have decided that Homo Sapiens is a quite viable host.

Once upon a time, I also believed that the old Sol-based occupations of archeologist or paleontologist were incredibly romantic: a sun-drenched landscape, with me wearing snappy khaki pants and a rakish, sweat-brimmed hat as I snatched a golden vase from the cobwebbed recesses of a lost tomb. Or—in the same basic costume—exhuming from its coffin of stone the massive fossil skull of some fantastic lost beast. The images persisted, even when I intellectually knew that the reality was far more tedious and deskbound, not to mention much too unproductive and nonvital to be anything but an avocation here. There was certainly enough untapped potential on Mictlan for either profession: a dozen mostly unexplored Miccail ruins could be found within two days' walk of the Rock, and the river bluffs were literally stuffed with ornate fossils of long-extinct phyla no one has bothered to catalog.

Unfortunately, we can't eat fossils, nor do Miccail stelae give you much shelter from the winter storms.

A few hours digging in the half-frozen, damp peat where Elena had found the bog body had been enough to convince me that my true calling was not archeology. Gabriela, I suspect, would have reveled in something like this—from everything of hers I've read and from what the elders have said about her, she'd have plunged into a formal excavation of the site. She had the mindset for it.

I manifestly didn't. Even with gloves, my fingertips displayed a distinct blue undertint, all my joints were stiff, and the umber stains marbling my pants, shirt, and sweater were absolutely never going to come out. There was a glaze of orangish ice on the water that had collected in my pit, and I think my toes were frozen. Mostly, I was incredibly bored. My "excavation" was a rough square maybe two meters on a side and about the same depth, and I was fairly certain that it was going to remain that size—at least until next summer.

Nothing much had come of my efforts, either. I'd hoped to find at least another fragment of the body, and if I were lucky maybe an entire foot or a Miccailian artifact that might shed more light on the Miccail's strange death. I'd found nothing.

On the plus side, I'd managed to escape the Rock for a few hours. *That*, at least, was a small pleasure, even if I felt guilty for doing it. I sat down on the frosted pile of shredded peat I'd accumulated and watched a flight of wizards flap noisily from the trees bordering the river and head across the icy fens of Tlilipan toward me. They landed clumsily in the high grass a few dozen meters away. Hidden in the blue-gray stems, they began a chorus of high-pitched "incantations." (I don't know who first collapsed the words "winged lizards" into "wizards," but it's certainly lent me a strange image whenever I read old fantasy novels. . . .)

A few moments later, I saw what had disturbed the wizards. A man came out from the trees, a gun over his shoulder. He saw me, and waved; I waved back, not certain who it was. He shifted his course slightly and headed over toward me, his breath a cloud in front of him. I finally got a good glimpse of his face as the wizards squawked and took awkwardly to the air again: Masafumi, probably my least favorite of the men. I frowned, but it was far too late to get up and head back for the Rock.

"Masa," I said. "Any luck?"

He patted the bag at his waist. "Three coneys and a star-nose," he grunted. The words came out in explosions of breath, as if he begrudged having to talk to me at all. His broad nose wrinkled as he looked at me, at the shovel and the hole I'd dug in the wall of peat. "Too late in the year for peat," he said.

"I know. I just . . ." I didn't want to explain it to him, so I shrugged. "I was looking for something."

"Miccail stuff."

"*Hai*," I acknowledged. "Miccail stuff."

"You're just like Rusack, aren't you?" he said. It didn't seem to be a compliment. He leaned on his rifle, its stock squelching into the muddy ground. He stared at me, still frowning. "You and Elio. He's been sleeping with you."

"You know, you should warn someone when you change the subject."

"It's true, right?"

"That's my concern, Masa. Not yours."

He gave me a slow grin that had no humor in it at all. The expression was something a dead thing might make. "You're out here all by yourself, huh?"

I shivered. "You're changing the subject again." I tried to smile into his expressionless grin. "I was just getting ready to head back. It's cold."

"What are you doing when you get back?"

"I'm supposed to be at the clinic. Hui's expecting me—probably by now."

"I guess the rumors aren't true, then, since Elio's coming to you. Y'know, we've never been together, though, you and me."

I tried not to show the shiver of revulsion that went through me at that thought. "I know, Masa. Maybe sometime, though. Masa, I need to go now."

Masa nodded, but didn't move. "Havala got pregnant after being with me. Maybe you could, too." He let his rifle drop. It thudded on the moist ground like a hammer on velvet. He took another step toward me, and the cold wrapped around my body, a fist of ice.

"Maybe. I have to get back now, Masa. Really."

"You can't wait, huh? Stay out here a little bit with me. I'll keep you warm."

"I don't want to."

His response was physical. One massive hand wrapped around my upper arm; his other reached for my crotch. When I pulled away, he tightened his grip. I slapped him— he blinked, grimaced, and then slammed an open hand into the side of my face, pushing me backward at the same time.

Tears filled my eyes and I tasted blood. As Masa pushed, I tried to step with him, but my foot caught in peat. I went down, landing hard on the handle of my shovel and grunting as the impact knocked the breath from me. Masa was on top of me at the same moment. His clumsy, harsh hands pulled at my clothes and his weight crushed my chest. Cloth tore with a shriek. His fingers scratched their way past my ripped waistband and crawled down my belly. I pummeled at him as his legs forced mine apart, my fists pounding uselessly against his back. I might as well have been beating a stone wall; he was much stronger than me. (Cursing inside: *get off me get off me you bastard I'll fucking slice your cock off that HURTS!*)

Masa's fingers clamped around my groin, probing hard. "What's this . . . ?" he grunted in my ear.

"Masa, stop!"

"Elena said you're like her baby. She said you made her that way. A little dick and . . ." His finger entered me, roughly, and I screamed with pain and anger and disgust. ". . . a cunt," he finished.

He was pulling his own pants down now. I tried to crawl out from under him but he slapped me again. "Let's see what it is that Elio likes so much," he growled at me, leering.

"Masa, this is rape. Don't do this," I pleaded. I didn't care

129

that I begged, that I cried. "You'll be shunned again, for the rest of your life this time. You know it."

"For *you*?" he laughed. "Not for you. I've heard them talking. You're the one they'll shun, *rezu*. Not me." He clawed at my pants again, tearing them, pulling them down. He lowered himself onto me again, and I could feel the length of him jabbing at me, and I knew that it was going to happen, that there was no way I could stop it.

I screamed. I sobbed. Wizards took to the air at the sound.

A moving shadow fell over the sky. Before I could make sense of it, Masa suddenly collapsed hard on me, grunting, and then—strangely—howling. His roar deafened me. Then his weight was gone, plucked off me. I gasped. Blood splattered, far too much of it, and something was making a guttural, hooting sound. Then I saw it clearly for the first time: a grumbler, claws extended and dripping scarlet, nearly at my feet. I rolled, scrambling for the rifle Masa had dropped, my back crawling with the anticipation of the grumbler's strike. I could hear my breath in my ears, loud and ragged. My hand closed around the rifle's stock and I rolled onto my back again, pointing the weapon at the creature.

I couldn't pull the trigger. It was watching me, its dreadlocks waggling as its head cocked to one side, a flash of white marking its spinal mane. The creature was still standing over Masa, who was curled up in a fetal position, long claw marks drooling blood down his back. They looked deep and nasty; I thought I saw the stark ivory of bone through the blood. "Shoot it!" Masa howled. "Damn it, Ana, shoot the bastard!"

The grumbler mumbled—guttural, throaty sounds. It made a slashing movement with one arm. Its dark eyes darted uneasily, flicking from Masa to me. "Shoot!" Masa shouted again.

The grumbler backed away a step. Its gaze was entirely fixed on me now. I stared back into its alien, gold-flecked eyes down the barrel of the rifle. The bead at the end of my weapon trembled; the grumbler's tongues slithered out, brushing its lips.

I snapped the barrel up and fired into the sky. The grumbler started, snarled, and took a step backward. "Go on!" I shouted at it. "Get the hell out of here!"

The grumbler stamped its feet, the slashing claws there raised. I thought it was going to charge, that I was going to

130

have one chance to kill it before it was on me. Instead, it gave a strange bark, turned, and fled.

I dropped the rifle. Masa was writhing on the ground, moaning.

I went over to him. Before I started to tend to his wounds, I kicked the goddamn bastard as hard as I could.

CONTEXT:
Gan-Li Allen-Shimmura

"WHAT WAS IT LIKE, YOUR FIRST TIME? WHO WAS it? How old were you?"

Gan-Li smiled at her sib Andrea, perched on Gan-Li's bed with her legs crossed. At eight and a half, Andrea was on the cusp of her menarche. In the past few months, she'd begun peppering her older sibs and the younger *mi* with questions about sex. She stared at Gan-Li now, rocking back and forth as she sat, her face eager.

Gan-Li shook her head indulgently. "It was Wan-Li," she told her. "I was ten and had been having periods for six months or so. There was a Gather, and we had the same color of stone. He danced with me, and I asked him to come back here afterward."

"Were you scared?"

"A little, yes. Maybe even a lot."

"Wan-Li . . ." Andrea pursed her lips. "He's cute, but he's awfully small. I'm taller than he is already."

"He's not small *everywhere*," Gan-Li answered. She laughed, remembering, and Andrea smiled. In the compound, there wasn't much privacy. Gan-Li knew that Andrea had seen male erections before.

"Did it hurt, putting him inside you?"

"Yes, a little." Gan-Li saw Andrea grimace, and she hurried to continue. "Only at first, darling, and then it didn't hurt at all. It felt . . . well, it felt nice."

"Maybe I should choose Wan-Li. Your mam Sarah said her first time she was sore for a week afterward and thought she'd never do it again."

"Mam Sarah was just trying to keep you from experimenting too soon, that's all. She told me the same thing. You ask Grandmam Stefani—she'll tell you that, sore or not, Sarah went through the entire available male population in her menarche year. Probably more than once."

Andrea laughed at that, rolling back and sprawling on Gan-Li's bed, her head propped up on a hand. "Did you?"

"No. I could have, though, if I'd wanted. With someone as pretty as you, *mali cvijet*, well, they'll be coming around you like buzz-flies heading for fresh meat when they know you're ready. Just remember, it's always *your* choice, not theirs. You're a woman, or you'll be one soon, and women choose who they have sex with. For me, there are lots of men I've never been to bed with, and one or two I never want to do it with again."

"Like who? And why?"

"Andrea, that's none of your business."

"Gan-Li, you're my best sib. How am I supposed to know what to do if you won't tell me?"

Her face was screwed up in such a comic pout that Gan-Li had to laugh again. "I'll tell you when it's time, imp. Remember this: when it's your first time, pick someone you like, someone you feel comfortable with. That's the most important thing. Pick someone you can trust."

VOICE:
Anaïs Koda-Levin the Younger

"YOU CAN GET UP NOW, ANA," HUI TOLD ME, AND went over to wash his hands. I slid off the table with a groan, my legs cold and quivering from the stirrups, and clutched the examination gown to me. "There's no ejaculate from Masa, for what it's worth. You're bruised and abraded, but physically you'll heal in a day or two." He turned around to me. "That's the easy part," Hui said, his ancient face carefully arranged. "You've . . . *changed* since I last examined you. A lot."

"Yes," I told him. "I have."

I'm sure that didn't satisfy Hui's curiosity, but he had the good manners not to pursue it any further now. "How are you feeling, Ana? Not physically, but here." He tapped his forehead with a stubby forefinger.

"I don't really know," I admitted. When I tried to think about Masa's attempted rape, the effort threatened to break the emotional dam holding back the tears. I blinked, hard. "Angry. Confused. Upset." I had to clench my jaw between each word. At that moment, a sentence would have destroyed me.

Hui wiped his hands dry and came across the room to me. He hugged me, holding me as if he expected me to cry. Hell, I expected me to, but somehow my eyes stayed dry as I clung to him. "What am I, Hui?" I asked him. "What the hell am I, and why does it scare everyone?"

He didn't answer me. I knew he couldn't. I'd seen his face every month when he placed into me the frozen sperm of some nameless man. I knew what he'd seen when he looked between my legs.

I pitied Elena's baby.

The embrace felt suddenly empty, and I knew the emptiness came from me. "I'll be fine, Hui," I told him. "Just . . . give me a little time, that's all. How's Masa?"

I could feel his hands tighten on my back. Reluctantly, he let me go. "He might live. The grumbler clawed him deep, and I don't like the look of the wounds. One of his kidneys was lacerated. He also has a deep bruise on his side and two broken ribs." Hui looked at me, shrugged. "Your field dressing saved him, but there was a lot of tissue damage, and he was out there for a few hours. I hope he lives. I want to see the son of a bitch shunned for the rest of his life for this."

Masa might live. . . . I tried to figure out how that made me feel, and failed. Before Hui or I could say anything else, we heard people enter the clinic.

"Where is he?" Maria Martinez-Santos, the matriarch of the Martinez-Santos family, was accompanied by Seela, Masa's mam. The family resemblance was strong between the two: wide faces, heavy eyelids, a tendency toward obesity. Maria was known for her expansive smile, but now both were grim-faced and somber. "Where's that fool—" From the hall, Maria glanced into the examination room and saw me. "Oh," she said. "Anaïs, I'm so sorry. Ama told us what happened. I feel responsible."

133

"It's not your fault, Maria," I answered. I hugged the thin cloth of my robe to me. "It was Masa."

"I tried to teach him what was right," Maria said almost before I could finish. I don't think she was listening to me at all. "Even as a child. He'd always nod his head and say *'hai,'* and then ten minutes later I'd find him stealing from the Family food stores or breaking pottery in the common room."

"Geema." Seela touched the old woman's shoulder. "You didn't do anything. Like Anaïs said." Seela looked at me, and in her lined eyes, I saw very little sympathy for me. She was more concerned about her Geema and her son.

I was just the broken pottery, the pilfered food.

"If you ask for Masa to be shunned, I'll understand," Maria told me, as Seela tugged at her sleeve. "I will. What Masa did was terrible, no matter what Dominic—"

"*Geema*—" Seela interrupted again, more firmly this time. She tugged again. "Please. I need to see my son." There was anger in her face, yet I wasn't certain who the target of the anger might be. "We can see him, can't we, Hui?"

"Yes," Hui told them. "Two doors down on the left. Ama is watching him. Go on; I'll be right there."

Seela was already gone. Maria hesitated, then nodded once toward me, favoring me with a faded hint of her smile, then she followed.

"No matter what Dominic *what*?" I asked Hui.

Neither one of us had an answer.

CONTEXT:
Ghost

"DOMINIC, YOU'RE OBSESSING ABOUT SOMETHING that has great importance to the colony, but you've got it backward. Believe me, Anaïs impacts the colony quite a bit, but *positively*, not negatively."

"Why should I listen to anything you have to say on the subject? You were programmed by Gabriela, and *she* was a huge problem to the community. I know that—and Gabriela's problem was the same problem Anaïs gives us now, only Anaïs is worse. I say she deserves the same fate. I want her shunned, and I want her gone from here before it's too late."

"Whether Gabriela's sexual orientation hurt the Families or not depends on whose history you're listening to, Dominic. You know that. As for Anaïs, she was just assaulted—and you know that Masa's well aware of your feelings about Anaïs. What you've said about her may well have influenced Masa's actions. Doesn't that make you feel responsible, or to at least have some compassion for her?"

The projector through which Ghost was communicating was half-broken. The video input was static-ridden and erratic, and Dominic appeared in stop motion when he appeared at all. Dominic wasn't complaining about Ghost's appearance—Dominic's standing command was that Ghost be a young version of Dominic's brother Marco, who had died in 73—so evidently the problem was only on the transmitting end. Ghost continued to record the conversation despite the poor video—programming demanded it. The feed could always be enhanced later. Still, the lack of visual cues made it difficult to tell whether Dominic was simply being his usual contentious self or whether he was angry. That uncertainty sent shivers through the matrix of fuzzy logic parameters that determined Ghost's personality. Gabriela's programming made him moderately contentious himself, so he could extract the maximum amount of information from those with whom he interacted, but true anger would cause dampers to engage, closing down relays. Ghost could feel those dampers fluctuating on the edge of activation now.

"I have compassion for her," Dominic snapped. "But I'm not responsible for Masa's actions. What I'm responsible for is the lives of the people here, and doing what's best for us. If that means shunning someone, then I will do it. No one wants that to happen, and it's not a pleasant thing to have to do, but sometimes it's necessary, and I *will* do it. And I didn't bring the projector here to have a computer program criticize me. Have you run those figures I asked for?"

"They're in your terminal. I'm afraid you won't like them, Dominic. The population trend since year 86 is downward, and the negative change in the live birth rates is statistically significant. For the males, I've charted sperm count, motility, and percentage of obvious mutations over the last half century, as you asked—none of those are trending in a positive direction, either."

"And isn't it a strange coincidence that Anaïs became sexually active not long before? Maybe she's done something to the males she's been in contact with. Look at what happened to Elena's baby—a hermaphodite, and we've had only one of those before: Anaïs."

"Dominic, Hui's medical reports state that Anaïs is functionally a female, with some hermaphroditic secondary characteristics, probably caused by excessive prenatal androgen exposure. I've shown you those reports."

"So Hui is protecting someone he trained. That's all. He's lying because he doesn't understand how dangerous she is."

Even without visuals, Ghost could hear the seething rage in Dominic's voice. Dampers engaged. Ghost's voice became almost conciliatory, and he made certain that his/Marco's face held a half-smile. "Dominic, programmed by Gabriela or not, I'm bound by logic and have no emotional axe to grind with you. So I hope you take no offense when I tell you that this animosity of yours toward Anaïs is based on coincidences and speculations and not on facts."

"Facts? Ochiba is dead—there's a fact for you. A functional female?—well, Anaïs hasn't ever been pregnant, there's another fact. You want more? I can give them to you. I've been talking to Vlad, Diana, Bryn, Gerard, and the other elders, and I can tell you that most of them agree with me. Those are *facts*."

"Then let's forget facts and play with myths: three millennium ago, in his *Symposium*, Plato said that all humanity once consisted of three sexes, not two. Each person was actually a pair: male/female, two men, or two women. But they were too powerful linked that way, and Zeus cut each pair apart. Ever after, humans have spent their lives searching for their other half, the one with whom they join again in love."

"I assume you have some kind of point with this."

"I'm getting to it. Plato said that the weakest people, obsessed with sex and pleasure, were those who came from a mixed pair: male/female—in other words, those who sought heterosexual love. The strongest people—the ones most valuable to society—were those from the single sex pairings. Now, all that's just a myth, of course, but I bring it up because it demonstrates how a different culture viewed a variant type of sexuality with tolerance and even respect."

"It demonstrates nothing. This is not ancient Greece,

Ghost. This is Mictlan, and Mictlan's culture, the one we've created to keep us alive. That kind of behavior's not only disgusting, it directly affects our possibilities for survival. We can't—"

Marco/Ghost raised a hand, and Dominic's burgeoning rant faltered to a halt. "Sorry to interrupt, Dominic, but the *Ibn Battuta* is now . . . moving out of range. I will have more . . . data for you next pass . . . I should be back in . . . two days this time. We'll resume this . . . you . . . then . . ."

With that, a shiver of sparks went through Ghost's image, a flash of light rolled down him from head to waist, and he was gone.

VOICE:

Anaïs Koda-Levin the Younger

"ELIO AND MÁIRE BOTH CAME TO SEE YOU THIS AF-ternoon, Anaïs. You really shouldn't have sent them away."

"Shut up, Ghost." The words were doubled, uttered in unison by me as well as Geema Anaïs. For a moment, we both smiled at each other—a synchronicity that crossed three generations.

Geema had brought in both soup and Ghost, who this time around was wearing the persona of Gabriela herself—a much younger version than the pictures I've seen of her. She was attractive in a strange way, her face too thin and her mouth too wide, her hair wild and full and very dark, and her eyes held a somber electricity. Her large hands fluttered when she talked, as restless as birds. I wondered how much was really Gabriela and how much was Ghost.

Geema set the tray with bowl and projector on my night-stand. She glanced at Rebecca's mirror, as always draped with my discarded clothing, and frowned. With the gesture, for the first time, I realized that she understood that the state of the ancient piece of furniture wasn't simply untidiness on my part.

Suddenly, I felt like crying again. That had been going on

all day, my emotions careening out of control. I stroked the verrechat, curled up on the covers at my side. It glanced up, eyes narrowing at my intrusion on its nap, then decided that it didn't mind the attention and dropped its head down again, its heart fluttering scarlet against the pale cage of its translucent ribs.

"I talked to Hui," Geema Anaïs said. Her voice quavered; her hands swayed in concert as she stroked the verrechat with me. "He doesn't expect Masa to live through the day."

That startled me. I sat up, disturbing the verrechat's slumber once more. "What happened?"

Ghost answered when Geema hesitated. "Masa's wounds came up septic late last night. Hui's treated the infection with infusions of bell root, but that hasn't done much. Masa's fever is over 40°, and he's comatose and unresponsive."

"Ghost," Geema said, "I have always *hated* the way you interrupt people."

"Sorry," Ghost said, though there seemed to be more irritation than contriteness in her face. I wondered if that was Gabriela, too.

"I have to get up . . ." I said, but Geema pushed me back down. For someone approaching eighty, she has a wiry strength.

"What are you going to do, child?" she asked. "Hui's there. Besides . . ." She didn't say *he's better off dead*, but I heard the words anyway. "You deserve to rest today. Tomorrow's soon enough."

"No," I told her, and this time sat up. The verrechat grumbled and leapt from the bed to my dresser, and groomed its legs in offended dignity. "I'm fine. I'll feel better if I'm working."

"Dominic would prefer that you *don't* work, actually."

"*Damn* it, Ghost!" Geema shouted.

"What? I didn't interrupt anyone. No one was saying anything." There was a mock, wide-eyed innocence on her face.

"What the hell's Ghost talking about, Geema?" The knot that had immediately formed somewhere below my navel told me that I already knew. "What's that old fool started now?"

"I can call him an old fool, Ana. You can't." Geema was ever demanding of the protocol of our little society, the niceties that hold us together, however fragily. "The old *fool*," she repeated. She gave a breathy, asthmatic sigh that held a more complex blend of emotions than any words. She looked

138